IN TIMES LIKE THESE

IN TIMES LIKE THESE

MAUREEN DUFFY

A FABLE

ISBN13: 978-0-9576020-2-1

PROLOGUE

'At all costs we must preserve the Federation,' the Chair says. We decided, or I should say it was decided before my time, that, in the interests of our commitment to complete equality the Chair should be a function not a person. So the Chair rotates between the First Ministers.

'If they want in it must be on our terms; that must be absolutely accepted from the beginning. This isn't a negotiation. They want us not we them.'

'We've done alright so far without them, once we got it and us together.'

'They'll want a negotiated agreement. You know they will.'

'You can't negotiate with 'perfidious Albion'. Centuries of diplomacy have made them too good at it.'

'As long as they leave it to their executive, not the politicians who'll want to bully and bluster.'

'I still think it's too dangerous,' Cornwall says. 'I say let them stew. We've got our alliances, our partnership with the Mid Europe Treaty, the MET, and the whole EAS. They'd never accept that!'

One of the failings of committees is a weakness for acronyms.

'And what can they offer: the Heptarchy, that could fall apart any minute.'

' What's that? The Heptarchy?'

'That was England, lots of little warring kingdoms 'til Alfred banged their heads together. That's what I call them now.'

'You and your history Cymri. I like to live in the here and now. I say we should try to pick them off one at a time till there's only Westminster and the Shires left. Berwick for a start. They'd jump at it.'

'It would make it harder for us; surrounded by the sea with an angry Southshire to the East.' Cornwall is clearly nervous.

'Well, it's clear we won't have a decision today. We have to go back and consult.'

'Suppose they ask to be let back into the EAS or even team up with MET themselves?'

'No one would trust them again. Don't you see: that's why they're asking to join the CF. It's a backdoor, as they see it, for something they should never have left, and find they can't do without!'

'But they're not Celts!'

'Historically neither is anyone. It was all a bit of Roman name calling, when it wasn't Brits or Scotti. But genetically, mitochondrially they are.'

'So we're told. And anyway we're all a mixture patriarchally. Let alone the latecomers from all over the world!'

'We have to hang on to something, know who we are.'

'We're human. That's all we know for sure.'

'And where we live.' Ulster says. 'That 's important.'

'That's the greatest accident of all.'

❧ ❧ ❧

PART ONE

AD 600

S o when he saw from where we watched on the flat top of
Ben Bulben, for Colm always had the power to see events
many miles away beyond the sight of most other men, the
dead lie in great heaps on the fields of Cul Drebne and, as
we afterwards learned, some three thousand had been slain
but only one of Colm's own clan, the Northern O'Neill, and
saw the great black flocks of crows like the pagan Morrigu,
settle on their bodies to peck out their eyes, then he knew
in himself he must look for penance from Molaisse, Abbot
of Devenish.

And this battle came about in two ways which I will
relate, for until we came to the Island of Hy and I was given
charge of the curragh and its passage between the islands, I
was always by his side as were the other eleven companions
who accompanied him here. This is the story as it was told
to me that when he was a student under Bishop Finnian of
Clonard, Finnian allowed him to see the psalter of St Jerome
that he had himself brought from Rome, and that was both
a holy book and a holy relic which the bishop kept privately

1

except when it was used as the custom is to teach the novices their letters, and how to read and write.

Not content with being allowed to study this holy book Colm, who was both a great reader and writer of all sacred texts, and also of the ancient lore of Ireland which he learned under the Bard Gemman, came secretly at night and made a copy of it. And this he was able to do with his right hand by the light of the fingers of his left which glowed in the dark with enough luminescence for him to write by, which he took as a sign that he did God's work.

How Bishop Finnian came upon the truth of what Colm had done was not told to me but he demanded that the copy should be surrendered to him which Colm refused. Then it was agreed between them that Diarmit, High King of Tara should be the arbiter and judge. But as well as having no love for Colm because the King was of the Southern O'Neill who were always vying with the Northern, Colm's clan, for supremacy in Ulster, and also because he still leaned towards the old ways of the Druids, Diarmit gave the judgement to Finnian with these words: 'To every cow her calf, for every book its copy'.

The second occasion of the conflict however was not over a book but a death and a violation of sanctuary, and it was that which finally led to the battle of Cul Drebne.

Curan, son of Aedh, King of Connacht, a Christian, was held hostage by King Diarmit at Tara. During a game of caman by accident he struck and killed the son of the King's steward and fled to Colm's church in Derry, he being a kinsman. Yet in spite of the holiness of sanctuary, and even the ancient laws of hospitality, he was dragged from there and murdered, and Colm himself was put under guard. Because Colm was not only a man of God, but a prince of his clan who could have been king himself if he had wished, he was deeply affronted. When in a rage his red hair seemed to flame and he himself grew even taller than his normal stature which was itself above most men.

Colm escaped from his guards and roused the men of Connacht and the Northern O'Neill. Diarmit marched North and met them at Cul Drebne. Before the battle the High King, who had appointed the pagan Arch Druid as his chief adviser, set his army to march widdershins around an ancient cairn while their priests marked out a magic circle around the King himself.

Nevertheless Colm's army was victorious through the power of the Lord. The King fled but the victors did not follow up their success. Then Diarmit brought a complaint to a synod convened at Teltown near Toru for Colm to be ex-communicated for sending so many souls to their death unshriven. However Colm was supported by his old master Bishop Finnian and the Holy Brendan of Clonfert and the attempt failed. But repenting of those three thousand dead in the battle, Colm asked the holy hermit Molaisse to be his confessor, and it was he who gave Colm this penance that he should leave Hibernia-Scotia and never return until he had converted as many souls as he had damned.

Accordingly and at the summons of King Conall of Dal Riata, his kinsman, who ruled the land we Scotti had taken from the Britons, we set sail for Britain in the curragh, twelve companions with Colm, and crossed the twelve mile strait in fine weather with God's blessing, to become exiles for Christ. And these were those who went with him as the disciples followed their lord and ours: Ernan, Baithene, Dermatt his constant attendant, Rus and Fechno, brothers, Eochaid, Tochann, Ciaran a King's son, Grillaan, and last myself, Luguid, who had then as after, command of the curragh.

So we landed safe among Colm's clan in Dal Riata at Kintyre.

✤ ✤ ✤

Now

'Well they're determined to do it,' Terry dropped her briefcase inside the front door. Seeing the room was empty she went on through the kitchen into Paul's studio. 'I need a drink.'

'Do what?'

'Go ahead with the referendum.'

Paul put down her brush, half turning towards Terry. 'What does it mean? I don't follow. Come and kiss me and explain.'

'It means,' Terry said, putting her arms round Paul and kissing her neck, 'that I'll have to go up to the constituency this weekend and talk to the committee. See what they want me to do.'

'But it's my p.v.'

'I know darling, and I'm very sorry not to be there, of course, but I don't have a choice.'

'I don't see why not. Can't it wait a few days?'

'We were whipped today. Told to get up there and take the temperature. See what can be saved.'

'But the party's against it.'

'That doesn't mean the members are or the voters. Just the leadership and us poor sods who'll be out of a job.'

'What do you mean?'

'No more Scottish constituencies at Westminster if the Union goes.'

Paul sat down in the battered wicker chair she kept beside her easel. 'It's serious then. I think I need a drink too. Get a couple of glasses. I'll fetch the bottle.' She got up slowly and went through to the small kitchen of the flat. Opening the fridge door, she stood for a moment looking in as if she couldn't remember what she had come for. Then, seizing the chilled bottle by the neck, she went back into the sitting room.

'Cheers!' she said as they touched glasses.

'Not much to cheer about.'

'Come and sit over here on the sofa. Now explain.'

Terry swallowed a cold mouthful of Pinot Grigio. 'If it goes through, I mean if enough people vote for independence, there will be no more of us in Westminster.'

'But do you think they will? The polls seem to say...'

'Polling's different from an actual vote. The tribalism will kick in. Psychologically it will feel like betraying the country, the people, the history, to vote against.'

'What about party tribalism? Isn't that just as strong?'

'Not as strong as nationalism. It would be a kind of rejection of the motherland, that sort of thing, even if reason said no.'

'And does reason say no?'

'Some does, some doesn't. The committed nationalists think they can go it alone with what's left of the oil and gas while they build up alternative energy sources, wind and wave that they've certainly got plenty of, and links with Norway, the feasibility of a North Sea pipeline or the discovery of new fields. Then there's coal that can be brought back into the mix; nuclear maybe. Government and EU farming subsidies could make the five million population practically self sufficient Then there's tourism, and the whisky exports to buy imports with.'

'So they could do it?'

'It'd be tough at first but it'd also generate jobs in the medium term.'

'But not for you. Couldn't you stand for the Scottish Parliament?'

'There'll be hundreds, seventy-three ex-Westminster for a start, trying to do just that and it's full up already.'

'You could stand for another constituency. What about Wales?'

'Darling your understanding of how and why people vote is so refreshing. You think it's about reason, common sense even, when it's more like supporting your local football club. The party will be decimated. I doubt if I'd even be selected, tarred with the national brush as a Scots traitor.'

'Well then, what will you do?'

'Go back to what I should, maybe, have stuck to in the first place, being an historian.'

'Teaching you mean. But you wouldn't teach in an academy. I know you.'

'No. I'd go back to FE or HE.'

'A university? Wouldn't that be just as hard to get now?'

'Not as an ex MP,' Terry paused, 'in the North.'

'You mean move up there permanently?'

'Would you?'

'It's a bit of a shock. Let me get used to it. Let's not talk about it anymore. Let's go to bed. You need a bit of TLC. We've still got that.' She leant towards Terry and kissed her. 'Bring the bottle.'

⚜ ⚜ ⚜

Paul was late climbing the stairs to the gallery above the pub where her work was on show. Flora, her agent and the gallery owner, would be going spare. The bar below was already crowded and she hoped some might find their way upstairs, driven by curiosity or just looking for the loo.

She had gone to Kings Cross to see Terry off, stifling a stupid feeling that she might never see her again, although Terry hated to be seen off at station or airport. 'What the fuck happened to you?' Flora said as she reached the top of the stairs. There were already one or two small groups of punters hovering by the drinks table or wandering round peering into the work, catalogue in hand.

'I had things to do,' Paul picked up a glass.

'Yes, here! Under the Microscope are sending their arts guy. Only on-line but it's better than nothing if he likes them.' Flora gestured towards the glass boxes on their stands. 'Be nice to him.'

'Depends how nice he is to me.' There was a clatter on the stairs.

'Hi Paul!'

'Hi!'

'Congratulations! Are we allowed a drink?'

Paul moved towards the new group. 'Well you're all over eighteen or you wouldn't be in my class. Thanks for coming anyway.' She raised her glass to the students. 'Cheers!'

'Where do we start? A tall fair boy in ripped jeans and paint spattered shirt picked up the printed catalogue sheet. 'What's it called?'

'De Minimus.'

'Oh classy, classical. Come on you lot. Bring your glasses. You're not here just to gossip.'

'Thanks Joel.'

'They're a faithful lot your students,' Flora said. 'They always turn up to give it body, like bums on seats in a theatre. Now this looks like the Microscope guy.' She moved towards the head of the stairs. 'Hello Flora Levinski. I'm the gallery owner.' She put out her hand.

'We're almost the same then! Florian Tempinsky, <u>Under the Microscope</u>. Is the artist related to the wallpaper lot?'

'Alas no. This is Paula Sanderson whose work I hope you're going to tell all your readers to come and see.'

Paul shook hands with him. 'Shall we just look round and then I'll have a chat to you if I may.' He set off round the space with Paul beside him. ' This is a new departure for you. Don't you usually show paintings?

'I'm doing a Picasso,' Paul said, 'having a go at everything.'

'Conceptual art's been the thing for years now: Isn't it time to move on? I would have thought painting is making a come-back; that it's perhaps not the best time for the change you've made here.'

'I suppose that's right if you think in terms of what's in, what's out, but I'm too bolshie, as you'd probably want to call it. I've always responded to what's immediate for me.'

'So what would you call these?' Tempinsky waved his hand dismissively at the stands of transparent boxes.

'I don't think I want to categorise them like that. I didn't name them in my head while I was doing them. In retrospect you can call them 'maquettes', dolls houses maybe, miniature sculptures.'

'Do they all have a message? This one for instance: "Little lamb who flayed thee." A corruption of Blake meaning…?'

'If you want a meaning you could say the agribusiness.'

'And Blake?'

'Poet and artist, so very much my hero. And of course with a message.'

'I thought these days "the medium is the message"?'

'Well, the internet's rather done for that, with its use of other peoples' messages.'

'And this one: Anteater, with just the animal standing on a green field.'

'You can say it's just a pun, fun, or a rejection of family tyranny.'

'A touch of father Freud there?'

'Isn't there everywhere?'

'Well it's been very enlightening talking to you. Thank you so much.'

'My pleasure.'

Flora hurried over. She had been watching out of the corner of her eye while she talked to a prospective patron, trying to gauge how it was going from body language.

'What do you think? Will he do something?'

Paula turned down her thumb. 'If he does we probably won't like it. Changing the subject: would you still represent me if I had to go to Scotland?'

'Why would you do that?'

'We might have to if Terry gets a job up there. I can work anywhere.'

'Would you still want to show here?'

'Of course. I couldn't expect everyone to come up there. Though I'd want to make new contacts as well.'

'But you're not one of them. It's difficult. I've noticed a trend towards the regional. Hockney's fault for making it fashionable: nostalgia. The English are always good at that.'

'Isn't everyone?'

'Suppose I got nostalgia for Kiev. That wouldn't go down well in Mayfair.' When she was excited Flora's perfect English took on a Slavic tinge.

'It would if you had an oligarch or two in tow.'

'You are such a cynic Paula.' Flora always pronounced it with an Italian lilt. 'Don't turn around but isn't that Kiril

Kravic, who's just come in. He never comes to such a small gallery!'

'I told you you needed an oligarch.' The room had suddenly filled up. Paul shifted slightly sideways so that she could see the door and glanced quickly across the press of bodies.

'And I am telling you not to look. I go and speak with him.' Already Flora was thinking in Russian. 'I bring him to you and you also speak. This is your big break-out.'

'Not unless he's better than the guy from <u>Under the Microscope</u>.'

'Please Paula. For me. Think of the gallery.' She began to push her way through the crowd whose voices were rising to be heard above each other as they sipped and chatted, occasionally peering down into one of Paul's glass boxes.

Flora had returned with a dark suited man in tow and his silver fur-coated partner. 'Kiril Kravic, Paula Sanderson.'

'If he asks me about wallpaper I shall walk away,' Paul thought.

'Will you please be showing your work Miss Sanderson. I am very interested. And my wife says I do not look too much at women artists. You are usually doing the paintings. Why you have change?'

'I still paint. It's just that somehow the times seemed to need a different response.'

'I have see your website. Your work is still, calm.'

'But not the times.' Paul moved forward parting the drinkers. 'This is the list. Is there anything you particularly want to know about?'

'I will see the ones in the middle please and you will explain. Then I can visit with the rest myself.'

Kravic had chosen well. Most people were still gathered by the door and the drinks table while a few were moving round the exhibits against the walls.

'Tell me please how you make these?'

'The glass boxes are from the same sources as the new showcases for medieval objects at the V and A. The figures come from toy shops, model shops and so on and then I work on them.' Paul always hated having to explain her work.

'And this one?' He moved towards the box in the very middle of the room.

'Jesus!' The woman in the fur coat said.

'What does it mean: 'Prime Cuts?' Kravic asked.

'That's the best pieces of meat from an animal; like steak for instance.'

Kravic stood quite still staring down into the small theatre where a figure in traditional butcher's apron and white cap had raised a bloody cleaver over a chopping block on which lay a miniature baby. Beside the table stood a basket half full of limbs, heads and torsos.

'It is political yes?'

'Yes.'

'It is very powerful. Now I will look at some more myself.'

Paul just managed to stop herself from bowing before she moved away after saying a muted: 'Please do.'

'How did it go?' Flora was at her elbow.

'Better than the last one, I think. He wants to look at the rest by himself, except the fur coat of course. I was afraid she was going to faint over 'Prime Cuts'.

'American,' Flora said as if that explained it. 'Get a drink. I have to circulate.'

Paul picked up a fresh glass and wandered over to where her students were going the rounds.

'You're always telling us paint's the real medium then you come up with this,' the class rebel said.

'Sometimes you have to step back from a particular medium to refresh it for yourself. Now I'm back to my brush. Before I did these I was feeling a bit stale. They've given me a new perspective shall we say?'

Out of the corner of her eye she saw Kravic, the fur coat and Flora pushing their way towards her. She turned to face them, moving a little away from the students who formed a natural backdrop. 'Like saints or angels in an airy skyscape hovering behind the main foregrounded actors,' she thought.

'Madam Flora speaks the perfect classical Russian we do not hear any more,' Kravic said. 'Your work is powerful. You do not ask enough for it. I take six pieces and make the small exhibition. These ones I have marked.' He waived the catalogue sheet at them. 'But I will ask much more to give them value to collectors.'

'And I'll get my 2% of that too as well as the actual price,' Paul thought. 'That's very good news. Thank you,' she said aloud.

'We shake on it.'

'Now you can't go hiding yourself away in Scotland,' Flora said when they had gone. 'This could be a real beginning for you.'

Something about choosing 'perfection of the life or of the work' surfaced in Paul's mind. 'We'll have to see,' she said. 'Anyway nothing may come of it. You know what the big boys are like. He may change his mind tomorrow.'

⚜ ⚜ ⚜

AD 600

Though we had landed safely at Kintyre it had not been without hazard in making the crossing for, though it is short as the crown flies, yet to round the point of the Mull is perilous because of the treacherous currents which threatened to sweep us away, and made the curragh difficult to steer in a straight line although all bent to the oars. For sometimes we would be whirled about as if the sea would drive us towards Corrievrechan, and the fatal whirlpool, the boiling cauldron that would suck down men and boats to the gloomy seabed where the demon lies waiting to imprison them together. Then Colm would lay aside his oar and standing fearlessly in the prow call upon God to protect us even as he protected the disciples when the mighty storm arose on the Sea of Galilee.

And directing the men at the helm, for it needed two and sometimes four to wrestle with the steering oar against the will of the currents, he drove the curragh forward until we rounded the point, and came into calmer water in the lee of the isthmus at Dunaverty, where we jumped ashore and dragged the boat up the beach of golden sand, until it was out of reach of the tides.

Above us towered high cliffs, at whose foot lay tumbled slabs of rock, and on one of these Colm stood, lifting up his hands to give thanks for our delivery from the waves. And it was seen when he stepped down from there that his foot had imprinted the surface so that it should always be known where he had first come ashore.

Then he said: 'Here we shall build our first chapel so those who come after to bring all these peoples to the true God, which is the Lord, shall do as we have done and cover this narrow land with His praise.' And after this was made true, for when others followed, as the friends of his student days, Cainnech and Comgall, they dedicated to God: Kilkenzie, Killdaloig and Kilmichael, as Colm himself first commanded us to weave branches and cut down posts for the chapel of Kilkerran, in honour of his friend Ciaran who would also follow after.

'For,' he said, 'we will go North to meet my cousin Conall who has need of us because the pagans press him hard. And besides if we should stay here our mission would not be accomplished to these same pagan Picti, whom Ptolemy calls Creanes and are one with our own Cruithneana of the North as I believe, and we should see the temptation of our own country across the water on fine days and yearn to go there, forgetting God and why we have come.'

So we stayed only a few weeks to prepare ourselves and build the two chapels before setting out to find the Taosearch Conall for he was not yet a Ri, a King, but only the chief of the Dal Riata Scotti. Taking again to the curragh we sailed along the right hand coast between that and the Island of Arran, putting in at night to cook a meal of fish and porridge and give thanks for that day's deliverance from the seas. At last coming to Tairpert we rested two nights before setting sail again up Loch Fyne.

Then Colm sent on ahead the youngest and fittest of us to warn Conall of our coming, which we continued by sea, and provided him with money that he might get himself a horse if any was to be had. At last we came to the head of the loch where we must leave the curragh and travel on foot, singing as we went the four miles to the fort of Dunatt where Conall kept Court, finding our messenger had indeed arrived before us and a place was ready where we could lie at night.

❧ ❧ ❧

Now

'Where've you got to?' Paul's voice said when Terry clamped the mobile handset to her ear.

'Just got in to Glasgow. Heading for the bus station. It's raining. How did it go?'

'Kravic, who's a wealthy gallery owner, bought half a dozen. Said he wants to make a mini exhibition of them.'

'Brilliant!'

'And I sold a couple to friends.'

'So a lot of red dots then. What're you doing now?'

'Going out with Flora and some of the students who dutifully turned up. Will you be okay?'

'I'm fine. I'll probably go down to the <u>Thistle</u> when I get to Dunoon.'

'Let me know when you're safely there. I always worry about the ferry. Miss you.'

'Miss you too. But it's not for long.'

'Hope there's a bus soon.'

'So do I. Just coming into Buchanan Street. Bye baby. Bye.'

Terry had emailed her agent to warn him of her visit. As the coach crossed the Clyde she wondered whether she should look up her old professor at Glasgow, now only emeritus but still with her finger in the academic pie, and sound her out about a job. It would be hard to go back to being a junior lecturer. Maybe she should try for an English or Welsh university; offer them politics as well as, or instead of, history. But perhaps these years at the coalface of Westminster had made her too cynical. She might be accused like Socrates, of corrupting young minds by telling them what it was really like: the backbiting, the jockeying for position, the smooching the great, and not so good, of energy companies and hedge funds.

How much did the public, the punters, the voters, really see or understand? Or were they just as cynical. She heard her father's voice saying: 'Never believe what you read in the papers. They're all a lot of shitehawks. They talk as their belly guides them.' She could imagine his response to the latest round of scandals, phone hacking, police corruption, handouts to officials, bedding down with politicians.

'Better, cleaner, to stick to history,' Terry thought as the coach ate up the M8 on its way to Greenock. The rain had stopped as they left the city. She was glad of the long light evening ahead. It would still be daylight when she reached the fisherman's cottage that gave her a legitimate foothold in the constituency, looking out across the Firth, a sea that in full sunlight showed turquoise, as if Paul had mixed blue and green on her pallet to foreground the seascape.

The coach bumped its way onto the pier at Greenock and then docked on the Western Ferry car deck for the short trip across the strait to Argyll she could already see from the passenger deck; the Boundary of the Gaels, she remembered, Dal Riata, Colomba's old clan. Well she would have to brush up on all that if she went back to academic life.

It was the professor who had suggested she try to stand for the constituency when Terry had first spoken of giving up teaching for politics.

'But we've never taken that seat.'

'Things change, especially in politics. John Smith went to school there. If he'd stood it might have been different. Historically it's an area that's always appealed to the romantic in you. And you've got the cottage. Maybe they'd like someone young and fresh...'

'And gay?' Terry said.

'That's changed too. And Paula's done some terrific paintings there. Give it a try Terry.'

'But I'm not Scottish.'

'But you chose to study at a Scottish university. That must make you a sort of proxy Scot. And you have the cottage.'

Terry decided to change the subject. Once Jane Sims got hold of something she didn't let go, rather like the small rough haired terrier who sat patiently on a chair in class while the professor lectured.

Once planted though the idea had grown on her. Terry had bought the cottage before she and Paula met, and while she was still at Glasgow, finishing her P.H.D., with the little money left after her mother had died in the care home where she had spent the last two years of her life after a disabling series of small strokes.

Perhaps it had been the sight of her mother, lying in a coma, her face fallen in because her teeth were in the mug on the bedside locker, that had made her buy the little ruined two-up, one-down, with its view across the Firth, in the first place, hoping to shut out that last image. And she had got it for a peppercorn or so it seemed to Terry used to London prices. She and Paula had restored the little house together to what an estate agent would have called 'presenting in an immaculate condition.'

Building on Jane Sims' suggestion she had begun to take an interest in the town and its people, joining the local party instead of being just one of the tourists the community relied on for its economy, now that it was no longer a fishing port as it must once have been, before becoming a destination for day trippers from Glasgow in the nineteenth century and even more famously the home of Sir Harry Lauder, or later, part of the hinterland of off duty resorts for American nuclear submariners based at Holy Loch.

As a lecturer at a redbrick university converted from the local polytechnic they could retreat to the cottage and while Paul painted Terry wrote and studied the history of their second home.

'What would you say if I said I was thinking of going into politics,' she had asked one evening after a local party meeting.

'I'd say go for it if that's what you want. But what exactly would you do? Try for Lambeth Council?'

'I was thinking more of Parliament. I just feel there's so much to be done. I'd like to have a go at some of it.'

'What does Jane think? She wanted you to apply for a senior lectureship.'

'I haven't discussed it with her. I wanted to see what you thought first.'

'Where would you stand?'

'Oh I'd have to get myself on a selection list somewhere. But I'll have to get better known in the party first.'

'Babe if that's what you want...'

So when Jane Sims came up with her suggestion and the existing candidate announced his retirement, Terry sounded out the local party.

'I can hardly believe it. They actually picked me,' she told Paul. 'Now I have to get elected so as not to disappoint people.'

'How long have you got?'

'Two years before the next electiont, unless the government falls before then.'

That had been five years ago. Now she put the plastic bottle of milk she had picked up on her way back, into the little fridge, phoned Paul to say she had arrived safely and set off for the Thistle to meet Jim McClellan, her agent.

'How's Paula?' he asked. 'Not come up with you?'

'It was the private view for her next show. I should have been there. But the word was I should be here. How's it looking?'

'A mess. Don't get me wrong: if it was left to this town there wouldn't be a problem. The first minister isn't popular here and neither are some of the people the locals think might get power with independence. If it went the way of the last Scottish Parliament it would be equally balanced with four in favour and four against. I have to tell you not all our own lot can be relied on to toe the line when it comes to the shove.'

'What about you Jim?'

'I'll do as I'm told. But then I've always been nervous about what W.B. Yeats described as: 'things fall apart, the centre cannot hold / Mere anarchy is loosed upon the world.' I'm from Galloway. My brother and I watched our father drink away the family farm. That was another form of anarchy. Thank God for this country's tradition of free education. It saved us from what could have been a life in the old 'underclass' as we're now supposed to call it.'

'I didn't have you down as a poetry lover Jim.'

'Ah well, that's another bit of my grammar school's bequest. It'll mean you going on the stump if we're to succeed here. You'll need a line of your own not just the party's to put across. Something to touch both the heart and the pocket. And there's an added complication I ought to mention.'

'Ok,' Terry said, 'don't worry I think I know what's coming and I'm ready for it.'

'Don't think it's anything to do with me or the way I think. We've always got on just fine and I admire and respect you. You've done a great job in the constituency. Everyone agrees on that.'

'Jim, spit it out. I promise not to throw a wobbly.'

'Okay then. It's religion and your being an out gay. The other side can appeal to both Catholics and Presbyterians that's why we don't encourage civil partnership here, let alone gay marriage.'

'Like Northern Ireland.'

'Not so extreme, but we've always been a bit inclined that way. It's so close across the water with lots of coming and going. Think of Rangers and Celtic, that substitute for real warfare.'

'It's too late for me to pretend, to try to cover up, but I'll keep it in mind. A pity my father didn't live in the manse.'

'Well, it didn't save Gordon so maybe it's not such a great advantage.'

'And the party line: 'greater devolution for all.' What do you think of that?'

'In theory it sounds good but it might just mean perpetual party dominance in distinct areas, always right or left. That could lead to corruption. Remember Liverpool on one hand and Westminster on the other.'

'You're a wise counsellor Jim. Maybe my line should be that we need Scotland to save, not just the whole union, but England in particular, save us from ourselves. And what we brought on ourselves with our own brand of racial arrogance and imperialism.'

Jim had arranged for her to address the party faithful the next evening. The Baptist Church Hall was already full when he led Terry onto the platform. Looking out across the room she saw row after row of tense and anxious faces. After Jim's introduction, 'she needs no introduction,' Terry moved across to the small wooden lectern feeling nervous and a little sick. How could she possibly reassure and win them over?

'First of all,' she began, 'I want to thank you again for the trust you showed in me at the last election, and for coming out in such numbers tonight. I hope in the intervening time you've felt I had your interests in the forefront of my mind, even though I was far away in Westminster, and that I was always accessible to you and ready to take up individual cases, as well as represent the whole constituency.

To say we are at a turning point for Scotland is an obvious cliché. Not so obvious is that it applies not just to here but to the whole union. You will know that the party has decided to oppose outright independence in favour of further devolution, greater independence without dissolution. I am not one of those who thinks this people couldn't go it alone. There is enough skill, tradition, commitment to education, to fairness, sheer nous, and natural resources for a nation of five million to make a go of it, though the scaremongers might suggest otherwise.

No I fear other things: a perpetual right wing government at Westminster, xenophobic and self-deceiving about its place in the world, a concentration on making a replica of Switzerland, a tidy sanitized southern state based on the financial industries, naval-gazing, complacent, to the neglect of the other parts of this island, and those who don't fit the stereotype – what I am asking is for the United Kingdom, Greater Britain to be saved from its worst tendencies by refusing to allow it to fall into its component parts and set them against each other.

How are those parts to be defined? I am an historian as many of you know. Looked at through the long telescope of history, fragmentation of this small piece of land doesn't hold up. Who are we; who do we think we are anyway? Even our own family histories have their surprises, the migrants, the name changes, the illegitimacies, the movements of whole chunks of populations. Where we are now, facing across to Ireland, is where so many of us have come from: the Scotti as the Romans called them, the Gaels of Argyll, their border against the Picts, and Galloway. Add in those same Picts, the painted people of the North, then the Vikings, the Britons from Strathclyde and migrating Angles from Northumbria, and you only have the first few waves of the mix. And the same is true across the whole island with the addition of Frenchified Northmen, continental Protestant refugees, Jewish, African, Caribbean, Asian and continental late-comers, and you have a Scotch Broth mixed with Lancashire hotpot, pottage and stew with a dash of curry and some black-eyed peas, that's our island's culinary pot-pourri as seen on the national screen.

Yet look at the DNA, at least on our mothers' side, and we're mostly Celtic stock, however divided. Here in this constituency we have a choice: do we go for the inaccurate mythmaking of a Hollywood Braveheart or the reasoned approach of Scotland's great age of the Enlightenment when it led the world in philosophy, science and innovation?

Do we want to abandon a process of integration begun by Colomba, carried forward by Kenneth McAlpin and James VI? We have a chance to find our own, new more equal way in the twenty first century, not of division, of fake nationalism, but respect and equality in harmony. The choice is ours.'

⁜ ⁜ ⁜

AD 600

The fortress of son of Comgill, at Dunatt is built on a rock like the Church of The Lord. On one side is the River Add and the great moss of Moine Mhor before the Sound of Jura. Had we known of the good anchorage there we would have taken a different, quicker though more hazardous, route by sea. As it was after we came ashore we made our way through the fields of oats and barley that feed those in the fortress, carrying the psalter before us and singing in procession. The fortress crag can be seen rising steeply above the fields, topped with the many buildings of Conall's court to a height of some 160 feet. There is only one narrow entrance where we were forced to climb up one at a time so that the whole can easily be defended from attack, but it would be hard to escape down the sheer rock sides if the fort were besieged or to sally out upon the enemy.

A great wall surrounds the buildings giving further protection with rooms for many people within the enclosures inside the walls. Conall at first received us courteously. But we had scarcely arrived when news came of another battle between the Cruithne and Colomba's clan, the Hy Neil, in which seven Kings of the Cruithne were killed and whether this news was brought across the strait, or Colm saw it in a vision, the King, Conall, was frightened by the power of the holy man for he had given his blessing to his own people, and they had made a great slaughter and the countryside between the Bann and the Bush was destroyed with fire. So I began to wish the power of Colm to be removed from Dunatt while Colm himself wished to begin to fulfil the task, which the Hermit Molaisse had laid on him, to convert as many pagans as the souls which had been slain at Cul Drebne. Therefore calling Colm before him Conall offered him a place where he could build a monastery, and be set on his way to the pagan, Pictish North. And the place that he offered was Hinba across the Sound which Colm at first accepted though that was not to be the place he would finally make holy.

So after a time when any who were not baptised had been brought into the fold, and lay priests left behind to serve the fortress, and Colm understood that he could do no more there, we made ready to remove to Hinba. But before we went Colm, noticing in a dry Spring that the cistern cut in the rock floor of the fortress to collect rain water was almost dry, left the fort by a little postern, and going down the hill, with several of us carrying spades, he ordered us to dig at a certain spot at the bottom. We had not gone down more than a few feet when water began to rise around our blades. Then Colm ordered us to build walls of rock slabs, for there the rocks are easily sliced into slabs of different thicknesses, and bigger stones to make a wall around the rim. To this day it is known as the Well of Colmcille and the water is always sweet.

Conall came with his band to see us leave from the mooring at Loch Crinan, which our party had reached from Dunatt in smaller coracles by the River Add, while I had been sailing the curragh down to Tarbert where we crossed the narrow isthmus by porterage into the Sound, and so up the Eastern coast of Knapdale. All embarked and took up the oars to sing our way across to Hinba while Conall and his men raised their weapons in salute.

After we had rested on the island for several days, knowing by his own restlessness that this was not the place God had intended for us to begin our work, Colm called us all together. 'This is not to be our home where we shall build the monastery,' he said. 'Conall son of Comgill offered me another island on the other side of the longer Mull. We shall go there as God wills.'

Then we were very relieved for the island where we rested was home to many wild deer, fierce in rut, who would eat any crops we planted to sustain us, and to adders which had been unknown in Ireland since St Patrick drove them away, as Colm would do from Hy in the year of his passing. So we made ready to leave again, rowing hard to keep from the maw of Corrievrechan which tried to suck us down while Colm stood in the bow denying it its prey with his prayers.

Keeping in the lee of the many islands for our own protection we at last crossed the Firth of Lorne to the coast of Mull and began our journey eastwards towards the setting sun. Then at the tip of Mull we crossed a narrow sound, trusting in God's will as made known to Colm that the island before us was indeed the pre-ordained place. But when our boat drew up at the nearest landing at the Southernmost tip of the island among smooth round rocks of many colours and Colm, jumping from the side into shallow water, waded up a pebbled beach and fell upon his face, stretching out his arms in the sign of the cross, we knew it was indeed the place. And that place was known ever after as the Bay of the Corracle.

⚜ ⚜ ⚜

Before

It was the title on the poster that had drawn Terry into the downstairs bar below the gallery: Scenes from Sappho. Looking round at the sparse clientele, two dusty building workers and an older man in a clean suit who might have been their boss or a local government inspector, she wondered whether she should have a drink first before following the pointing finger upstairs. Then catching the sound of laughter and the words: 'Stinky fingered lesbo,' from the group she moved towards the stairs, knowing three sets of speculative eyes would be following her progress.

The same poster was pinned to the door at the top, showing a woman seated in front of a mirror, a hand raised to her hair pinning in a flower. Across it was printed:

'You bound your brow with sweet smelling roses,' and then repeated again criss-crossing the image. There was no obeisance to ancient Greece. The girl in the picture was wearing a printed light top, figured in yellow, white and green, from a chain store, Gap or Whistles, and the leg curled round that of the chair was rough-textured denim blue. Terry pushed open the door and was struck, after the gloom of the stairs by a pouring of light from the long arched sash windows. The white washed walls were jewelled with the paintings and prints in amethyst, peridot, jade, topaz with all the delicacy of semi precious stones. Girls and women looked down from their frames, lay across the foreground or turned their backs, absorbed in their own actions and lives. Each was cross hatched with lines of verse. The room was empty yet seemed as crowded as a dance floor.

'There ought to be music,' Terry thought. 'It's as if you can hear voices, even singing, soprano, mezzo, alto.'

'Are you okay? Would you like a list. I'm Paula Sanderson.' She was holding out a single printed sheet of paper.

'Terry Ellis.' She held out her hand and Paula fumbled with the sheet of paper, finally settling for a left handed shake. Terry glanced down at the list.

'Have you been here before?'

'No, no I haven't. Shall I have a look round? It was the title on your poster drew me in.' She looked directly at the artist, knowing she was probing, flirting.

'You know the poems, well the fragments?'

'Some of them.'

'I think you'll find most of them here. It's my attempt to set her in a contemporary context. See what you think.'

Paula Sanderson moved over to the table just inside the door and began to sort papers then her phone rang and she walked out onto the landing. Terry could hear the deeper murmur of her voice as she turned towards the paintings and began to move from one to the other, checking them out on the list.

Girls sang, a woman lay staring up through a skylight at a rash of stars, girls danced, two lovers entwined naked on a bed, a woman sent another away weeping; the quotation read: 'I cannot share my bed with a younger woman', where the cross hatched repetition seemed to double the pain. And then she came to a portrait whose face was blank; just the outline of a head. Checking the list she saw: 'Anactoria?'

Paula had come back into the room. 'Why is Anactoria faceless?' Terry asked moving towards the table.

'Whoe'er she be, the not impossible she?'

'Could we meet, for a drink maybe. I'd like to bring some of my students to see your work.'

'Would they be interested?'

'I teach gender studies, and history, at the Met. They ought to be interested as part of the course. It would be good to discuss it over a drink. I should at least appear to understand your work more than the students before bringing them here.'

Paula laughed. 'You're very persistent. I'm here every day till six this week. If you dropped in about then we could have a drink downstairs. Or head out somewhere else if you'd rather.'

'Thursday okay?'

'Thursday. Paul had played a game in her head: heads she will, tails she won't. Then wondered why she had loaded it that way, but there the girl was on Thursday, on the dot of six.

'I just have to lock up and leave the keys downstairs, in case the place catches fire. Shall we have a drink here?'

'Let's go out.'

So they had walked into the beginning of Spring with pink and white prunus showering a confetti of petals around them. Afterwards they had laughed at the cliché. 'Why couldn't we have been more original and got off with each other in high summer or the dead of winter?'

They had found a wine bar near the law courts. Pushing open the door they were hit by a gust of competing male voices. 'Let's see if it's quieter at the back.' They settled at a corner table out of sight of the suits and began, with the help of a bottle of sauvignon Terry insisted on buying, to probe each other's past and present.

'Where do you live?' Terry asked, 'near the gallery?'

'No, miles away. Deepest South London, Camberwell or Denmark Hill, whichever turns you on. It's on the border. And you?'

'Like you, borderland. Battersea or Clapham. Depends on the estate agent and whether you're buying or selling. I've got a studio flat in a block. Rented. My great ambition is to buy, something: a dog kennel for instance.'

'Didn't you say you teach at the Met? That's a long journey every day.'

'It's not too bad: Northern Line to Embankment; then a few stops to Tower Hill. What about you?'

They were circling each other, looking for an opening, dancers whose hands didn't yet touch.

'Oh I'm mostly at home in my studio working, when I haven't got a show. Except if my agent's busy, I have to mind the shop like this week. I do a bit of teaching too, at Camberwell, but that's in walking distance.'

'You've got a studio at home?'

'It's a garden flat. When it's warm enough I can paint in the summer house. That's the best light. When it isn't it's the conservatory which is the rather grand name for a lean to at the back of the kitchen. I was lucky. In the great boom before London prices went crazy I was able to get a 95% mortgage, I'm still paying off of course. I did a mural for the local hospital that nearly paid for the deposit. You must come and see it – if you'd like to. I mean wouldn't find it dull.'

'Don't be daft. I'd love to. After all we're not that far apart.'

Afterwards they couldn't remember how they'd ended up in bed that first time, only their first kiss. And Terry had said: 'Is this alright for you?'

'I'm not backing away, am I.'

Then there had been the embarrassment of new nakedness.

'Take your watch off too,' Paul said. 'There's no time in bed.'

At first they had kept their separate flats, meeting when they could, both with other busy lives. Then Paula had said 'It's silly paying two costs, your rent, my mortgage. Why don't you move in? There's plenty of room for two.' And so it had happened with no big deal, just a quiet acceptance.

Then Terry had bought the cottage and there was a new element in their life together.

'How did your speech go?' Paul was asking now.

'Okay, I think. We'll only know when we get the result of the referendum. I think some people were a bit bemused, wondered if they'd wandered into a history lecture by mistake. Wish you were here.'

'Me too.'

'I'll be back on Thursday night. There's a vote I have to be in for on Friday morning. Then we've got the weekend. How about you?'

'Flora says she can do the weekend on her own. There's not likely to be another Kiril Kravic; just winding down.'

✣ ✣ ✣

AD 600

When we had rested and given thanks to God for our safe crossing and the curragh had been safely anchored to a strong stake driven into the shore we took from her such provisions and goods as we had been able to fill her with and the sledge on which we placed the heaviest such as the cooking pot and tools for carpentry and working the land. 'Now,' said Colm, 'let us explore the place that God has ordained for us which we may know from his bringing us here safely through the waters and past the demon whirlpool. From this small island we shall lighten all these northern parts if it is his will. Here we will build our church and our home in the eye of God with only the seas around us. Now let us find the promised spot.'

So we set out along the shore, dragging the sledge across the sand or carrying our other possessions on our backs. And at last when we had travelled two miles to the

North along the eastern shore, we turned a little inland to where the sea lay equidistant on either side and before us in a great turquoise arc. 'Here,' Colm said, 'we shall build our monastery with Dun I at our backs to shelter us from the winter wind.'

So we laid aside our burdens and went down to the shore to gather driftwood for a fire and dried grass to set it going which we did with a firestick and set the pot upon it, with barley and dried fish for a stew. And as we ate one of the brothers, Rus, began a hymn with which the other, Fechno, joined in, the sound going out over the water, mingled with the cries of seabirds .The old tales say they are the souls of drowned sailors but Colm would have none of it but said that God was merciful and would not condemn them to whirl about the sky mewing like hungry children.

Then that first night we lay down together for warmth, each wrapped tight in his robe and plaid, rising at midnight after the first sleep to say vigils, at six by the candle to say prime and then at dawn for matins, breakfasting on the remains of the stew.

'Now we shall all have a task and begin to build,' Colm said, and appointed each according to his ability to gather more driftwood and cut branches from the low bushes which, because of the strength of the winds are all that will grow on Hy, to build the hut where he would write and read. And others he sent out in the small coracle to catch fish, and yet others to inspect the slabs of pink and granite with which we should build the altar to God, stopping only for prayers and food.

Eochaid was skilled in this work, knowing just where to place the wedge and strike so that the rock came away in clean slabs ready to be laid. First he ordered a trench dug which we filled with boulders and mud between them and then he began to place the slabs, keying in the different lengths for greater strength until he had taught several of us his skill. Then when he saw it Colm took some of the holy water he had brought with us and blessed this altar we had raised to the Glory of God, calling upon him as He had blessed the Temple of Solomon to look down in favour on this first temple to Him in this land.

Then I made many journeys in the curragh to the mainland, with brothers to cut down posts and drag them to the shore where I would ferry them across to Hy to build the great house where we slept and ate, and others gathered withies to weave the walls and thatch for the roof, and then more to build our first church.

So the monastery began to take shape.

❧ ❧ ❧

Now

After they had kissed as they always did, reunited, Paul said, 'The news isn't good I'm afraid. There's a mood building up of 'Let them go. Who needs them. They're only a drain on the rest of us,' and 'Why do they think they're so special: we beat them didn't we.'

'Who's saying this?'

'The redtops of course but also Twitter and the opinion polls like those EFE are running.'

'Who the fuck are EFE.?'

'The new think-tank off-shoot of the EDF.'

'I might have guessed. I must be even more tired than I thought not to have spotted that, predicted it. Is anyone countering all this junk?'

'All the mainstream party leaders of course.'

'But nobody's listening?'

'It's like kids in the playground when they feel not wanted. They become resentful and aggressive, bringing down on themselves just what they really don't want in their heart of hearts. They want to be in the gang, accepted, appreciated. "If they don't want us well we don't want them," that's what's happening now, encouraged of course by those who stand to gain the most by the break up.' Paul said.

'Or think they do. It's turning back the clock, not just a couple of hundred years to the Act of Union but back to the medieval them and us, seven hundred years. Why?'

'A yearning for a warrior age in our mechanised, digitised times, for some sort of identity that isn't just bloodless Facebook? Turning everyday life into a great computer game where you zap the other on your doorstep.'

'I would have thought there were still wars enough to satisfy that,' Terry said.

'But they're a long way away, as unreal to most people as what's on the screen.'

'I must say I'm not looking forward to the House tomorrow with all this going on. A lot of the honourable members will be running scared.'

'Oh and just one more thing to cheer you up: the Daily Rail sees it as the perfect excuse to pull out of Europe with the Scots reanimating the 'auld alliance' with France.'

'Don't tell me anymore. Let's go to bed. I need comforting.'

Paul was first up in the morning, bringing two cups of tea to drink together.

'What have you got on today?' Terry asked.

'Flora and I are going over to the Gallery Kravic to see how he intends to display the pieces he bought. He wants them now but he can't have them till the end of the show.

His red stickers might encourage other people to shell out. I insisted on Flora coming with me. I think he might be a groper.'

'What you do for art,' Terry said suppressing a sudden flush of jealousy.

'It's okay darling. We're quite safe. I just didn't want there to be any misunderstanding. What about you?'

'Well we've got a vote later on. I'll just check my mobile.' She pressed the 'on' button and navigated to 'messages'. 'As I thought: a party meeting's been called in Portcullis House for 10.30. Somebody's panicking over what you told me last night, is my guess. I'll keep you posted. It may be a long day.'

Paul and Flora arrived at Gallery Kravic, a converted warehouse in Rotherhithe, at the same time, Flora still breathless from climbing the stairs at the Tube station. Inside the building had been completely made over to resemble any other commercial gallery from around the world: white walls, an ebony floor and stainless steel fittings.

'Mr Kravic will see you in his office. He's sending someone down to fetch you.'

'Here we go,' Paul said.

'Now Paula, be good. Remember this is your big breakout.'

Terry came up out of the wide mouth of Westminster station into bright sunlight. A gaggle of oriental students passed, blocking the pavement, following their guide's raised baton. Voices from every linguistic culture competed with each other around her.

'The Last Days of the Roman Empire,' Terry thought as she turned the corner into the embankment where Boudicca whipped up her chariot beside Westminster Bridge. 'Hello old girl. I know how you must have felt. I wonder if you even thought you could win or you just wanted revenge.' She pushed her way into the revolving door, flashing her pass at the guards, heading for the escalator that would carry her up out of the glasshouse of the atrium to the committee rooms above.

⚜   ⚜   ⚜

'What happens next?' Paul asked when they were both back in the flat

'The process you mean. Who knows? I imagine there's a committee of lawyers somewhere, or maybe the Privy Council, trying to decide how legally you unpick the U.K. It's never been done before or not apart from Ireland. They'll be looking at that of course. But this is different, an actual Act of Union that would have to be annulled, presumably by legislation. So Westminster has got to vote to get rid of a third of themselves and a chunk of this small island and its people, and share it with a potential enemy.'

'That's a bit extreme.'

'Looked at from here maybe. But remember the problems with Ireland in the Second World War, and whether that was a back way to invade Britain.'

'So how long have they got?'

'Well, there might have to be another referendum, for the whole country this time. There will certainly have to be an election; that's due anyway. Then negotiations between the two sides as to what to put into the legislation and what sort to use: primary or secondary, a Bill fully debated. I don't think they could do it with just a statutory instrument that both Houses agree to. Either way it'll be a bloody business. And there are all sorts of things to be considered. They'll want a defence capability and Trident out of Scottish waters.

They'll want to take over all the Highland regiments. That's easy because their allegiance is to the Queen, and they'll want to keep the Queen, her mother was a Scot after all, Glamis castle and all that. But one thing's certain: it'll take time, maybe years. Who knows: maybe the new Scotland Bill will be enough to calm things down. I'm starving, shall we go out or have a takeaway?'

'I'll ring Chopsticks. Let's stay in.'

⚜ ⚜ ⚜

AD 600

When we had been some few months at Hy and had taken many journeys in that region and the islands to strengthen the faith of the people of Dal Riata, and had established a scriptorium within the monastery, where Colm was often to be found dipping his sharpened quill into the inkpot and the little holders of the different pigments to make each page an image of Christ's beauty and of his world that he had created, and nearby the pestle and mortar for Diarmit, his attendant who was always beside him, to grind the pigments into powder, one day Colm said: 'It's time to begin our real work here among the Cruithneana who are still in thrall to their druids. We shall go to visit their King Bruide mac Bile, and he shall confirm us in our possession of Hy for the Lord.'

For at that time Hy lay on the border between Dal Riata and the Kingdom of the Northern Cruithneana, or Picti as the Romans called them, as they called us Scotti which we keep even here.

So taking provisions we set out on the long difficult journey in the curragh to cross to the other side of Britannia, going first round Mull by the east coast and across the Firth of Lorne, and so into the mouth of Loch Linnhe, travelling many days north and east, up the narrow river Lochy into the loch of the same name, and finally the twenty three miles of the dreaded Loch Ness itself, deep and cold, and the habitation of a monster whom Colm later tamed. For once returning from the King's fortress he told one of us to swim across the Ness to fetch the boat that was on the other side. Now it happened that some villagers were just burying the body of a man who had been badly bitten by the monster while swimming in the Ness. Nevertheless trusting in God and Colm, Lugneus stripped down to his tunic and plunged in. The monster resting on the bottom felt the agitation in the water above him and rose up in pursuit of Lugneus. Seeing this Colm, standing up tall on the bank and making the sign of the cross, called in his great voice that could be heard from mountain peak to peak: 'Go no further, nor dare to touch the man. Go back at once!' At which the monster drew back as if hauled in by ropes and sank down from sight. Then we all gave thanks to see Lugneus coming safe across the water towards us.

But also the Loch is subject to sudden squalls and storms enough to sink a boat down to the monster's lair so we were glad when we neared the head of the Loch and could see King Bruide's fortress of Craig Phadrich rising above the eastern bank. Leaving the curragh moored we set out in procession, Colm striding ahead while we followed with our voices raised in a psalm until we came to the gates of the fort. Then making the sign of the cross with the holy book in his hand Colm called out in a great voice: 'Open in the name of Jesus Christ!' And the sun coming out at that moment it was as if a shaft of light from heaven lit up the high white dome of his tonsured forehead, and all his hair in a flame so that the gate keepers were afraid of his magic and pulled back the bolts and we could enter singing God's praises.

When this was reported to the King the gatekeepers fearing for their lives said that the bolts had flown back of their own accord such was the power of the tall man's God. Then the King calling Colm before him begged him to tell him about this God and that we should stay in his fortress so that he could learn more and how he might have a share of it for himself against his enemies.

So we stayed many days while Colm instructed the king and he in turn confirmed Colm's possession of Hy and that he would not take it from him or allow others to do so. And the king was confirmed in his faith in Our Lord when it was further witnessed by him and all his household that Colm caused a white stone to float upon the water rather than sink. Colm had taken the stone from the river bed and blessed it for a cure of various diseases and when it was placed on the water again then it remained upon the surface for all to see.

Then though King Bruide did not banish the Druids from his court and accept the faith which would raise him up at the Day of Judgement and save him from hell nevertheless he gave Colm permission to go the length and breadth of the land, converting his people and setting up daughter houses wherever God directed him. Then he would have given him bracelets and rings of gold but Colm ordered that they should be melted down and, making with his own hands a mould of clay, he formed them into the cross of Our Lord, saying that all things should be brought into this service and not made into toys to flatter human vanity.

⚜ ⚜ ⚜

201?

The wild cheering from the other side seemed as if it would never end. 'What do they think they're cheering for,' Terry said to the backbencher beside her. 'They've just abandoned three hundred years of history.'

'It was a clever move to make it a free vote. It gave all the little Englanders a free rein. And to couple it with 'Out of Europe' rhetoric just topped it off nicely. Did you see the Bluetops headlines this morning? A complete exercise in xenophobia.'

'Totally predictable that they would run polls among their readers to put the pressure on their members today. And with the free vote the government can't be blamed for breaking up the country.'

'Order, order! The Prime Minister.'

Vaguely Terry heard the string of platitudes through the outbreaks of catcalls and cheers.

'The will of this House; the will of the people. The final answer to the West Lothian question.' Laughter. 'This is still Great Britain, still great. We wish you well as you try to go it alone...'

Suddenly a group were on their feet and Terry heard the strains of singing, taken up by more and more male voices.

'There'll always be an England
And England shall be free
If England means as much to you
As England means to me.'

'Order, order,' the Speaker tried again but the voices were now chanting: 'England, England, England...'

'Order, order.'

There was a sudden quiet. Then a voice shouted, a hand pointed from the government side. 'I see strangers!'

'Out, out, out!' The cry was taken up. The speaker banged with his gavel.

'I'm afraid I must ask all those representing a now potentially foreign constituency to leave the chamber.'

Terry stood up. 'Delighted Mr Speaker. This is nothing but a bear garden.'

'This House is now in recess. God help us all.' The speaker banged again. 'Remove the mace.' Once again the singing broke out as Terry made her way towards the door, aware that others were falling in around her, and behind them sudden shouts of 'To the Tower, the Tower, the Tower.'

She was pulled up just outside the door of the chamber by the chief whip. 'Dining Room A. 10.30 tomorrow. We need to talk this through.'

'I suppose we're still allowed in the Strangers' Bar, for tonight at least. What about a quick drink? I need one!'

'Why not?'

They crossed the Central Lobby and made their way along the short corridor with its fake mullioned windows and Pre Raphaelite murals of history paintings: old assemblies, old rebellions.

'Shall I miss this place?' Terry wondered to herself. At the open end of the corridor where stairs went up to the gallery and down to the terrace and meeting rooms, the policeman on duty saluted them in recognition.'

'Nobody's told security yet,' Bob Stiles said. 'I wonder if we'd get through tomorrow?' They went down the broad staircase with its heavy Victorian, conker shiny banisters and turned down the narrow corridor on the left. 'We're not the only ones, judging by the din,' Bob said. 'What will you have?'

The bar was nearly full. Terry recognised several of her male colleagues, and here and there a rare female MP.

'You should join us now Terry. You're eligible as a resident,' the sole SNP member said at her elbow, raising his glass in invitation.

'Sorry Jamie. I'm an old unreconstructed Leftie. You know: 'The world is my country,' and all that.'

'Tom Paine. Aye. And he was responsible for the most nationalistic country on the planet. America. Well, we're the real Left wing now since New Labour. You'd fit in nicely. Stand for the Scottish Parliament. We'll be needing to increase the numbers.'

'I think I have had it up to here with politics for now.'

'Ah, you never lose the itch once bitten. So what do you think of doing?'

'A nice quiet post in academe would suit me very well.'

'I hope that doesn't mean turning your back on us completely.'

'Don't forget I did my degree at Glasgow. I'm not thinking of selling up yet. Not till I've seen this through. Even from the sidelines.'

'Is this man harassing you?' Bob had come up with the drinks.

Terry laughed and reached for the glass held out to her. 'It's alright Bob. Only politically. He wants me to join his lot.'

'We can always find you a job Terry.'

'Thanks for the vote of confidence Bob. I'm thinking of giving politics a rest for a bit.'

Jamie, the nationalist, was still there. 'As a resident you could apply for citizenship. There's a lot of empty space in Scotland we're going to be opening up. Maybe you've a grandparent would give you dual nationality.'

'Sorry Jamie I just don't believe in all that business. I believe we came out of Africa a few hundred thousand years ago and spread all over the world. But we're still all the same species; that's why we can interbreed.'

'So for you we're all the same; culture, history, your country, none of that matters.'

'Not fundamentally, no. It only sets us against each other.'

'Well, if you'll believe that you'll believe anything. I'm proud of my country and I don't care who hears me say so.'

'You're proud of a fiction, a fairy story we all tell ourselves because we want someone, something to tell us who we are. And that's what you've seen in operation today. These islands are all peopled by mongrels: a mix of Gaels from Ireland, Proto Celtic Picts, Welsh Brythons, Teutonic Anglo Saxons, Norman French Scandinavians and Scander Norse, let alone all those who came after from all over the world and we are still coming. There's no bit of these blessed isles that isn't a Christmas Pudding mix. You're just lucky if you can find a piece of silver. Passing the Scotland Bill doesn't alter that.'

'How did it go,' Paul said turning away from her easel, palette knife in hand.

'Don't ask. Well it got through with the help of a lot of little Englanders, including some fellow traveller UKIP and BNP, heavily disguised as patriots.'

'So what's next?'

'After this shambles, and the mix of arrogance and sheer fucking incompetence, who can blame the Scots for voting 'yes'. What have you got on tomorrow?'

'Another visit to the Kravic to see my new gallery. He wants to talk about the future. Today was just a courtesy call with Flora. Want to come?'

'Of course. But I can't. Party meeting at 10.30. Oh darling, what a mess it all is. Can we go off somewhere for the weekend, just the two of us. I could do with a bit less life and more loving?'

'Don't you mean fucking?' Paul said, putting her arms round her. 'Let's do that.'

⚜   ⚜   ⚜

'There was a sameness to the glossy commercial galleries,' Paula thought as she waited for the sheeted glass automatic doors to let her in again, but on her own this time. Already she could see through to the high white walls, the discreet notices, the mahogany reception desk presided over by the pristinely smart young woman. She stepped through the tall columned doorway onto state of the art wooden flooring.

'I've come to see Mr Kravic.'

A flashed smile, soon extinguished. ' Oh yes. Your name please.'

'Paula Sanderson.'

'And you say you have an appointment. I'll just ring Mr Kravic's secretary.'

While she waited Paula looked about her, wandering towards the first gallery opening off the foyer. The room soared up, a high white cube with a sparse scattering of works so unlike the crowded displays she was used to in public galleries or her own usual space. Her glass boxes would be diminished by such a setting.

'Mrs Sanderson!' a receptionist was recalling her. 'Mr Kravic will be down himself in just a moment.' Her hushed tone suggested that monarchy or divinity was about to descend, attended by baroque cherubs on a cushion of cloud.

'My dear,' Kravic appeared round the corner with outstretched hands hurrying towards her, and Paul found herself embraced and kissed. ' You are alone. No duenna today? Let me first be showing you where I intend for your beautiful works and then we will go to my office for discuss your future.'

Paul began to feel she had strayed into a popular, all pervasive television advert, and at any moment might find that she and Kravic had sprouted sharp noses, claws and greyish fur, while they propounded the merits of their insurance policies in fetching broken English, as Kravic led her through a series of vast, sterile rooms until they came to a smaller cul de sac.

'Here I would to put them on pillars for easier see.'

'That looks a good space,' Paul said.

'I would make the group of different heights so peoples can look up and down. There could be a theme, a progress if you would like it and you would write piece in catalogue to explain.'

'I think we could work something out.'

'Good. We go now to office. You drink coffee or wine, whisky?'

'Coffee please. Too early for me to start on alcohol.' Paul found herself being careful not to fall into his infectious pseudo-slavic idiom.

'We take lift. I order coffee when we go to office.' Kravic led her back towards reception. 'Please,' he stood aside at the open lift door, ushering her in with a little bow and regal wave of the hand. Paul felt layers of carefully nurtured independence being shorn away. She hoped she wouldn't be shut alone in the lift with him for long.

'Please,' he said again with his little bow towards the opening door.

'I think you should lead the way,' Paul said. 'You know where we're going.'

'If you wish.'

His office was plush with thick pile carpets, mahogany panelling, sunken lights, pictures in heavy gilt frames. Suddenly she was reminded of Manchester Town Hall and nearly laughed out loud at the contrived opulence, imitating the proud civic aspirations of the Victorian cotton mill masters.

'Please to sit.' He was waving her to a redly upholstered armchair. Paul sat while he ordered coffee, wondering how soon she could leave and feeling relief at the knock on the door that signified the arrival of coffee and another human presence. Too soon the tray was put down on Kravic's desk and the girl who had brought it dismissed.

'Milk, sugar?'

'Just milk, thank you.'

Kravic came towards her holding out a cup of dark coffee and a small delicate milk jug, Paula thought must be bone china by its chalky sheen. She took the cup and reached for the milk but Kravic held it just out of her reach.

'You must allow me. Say when.'

'That's fine thank you.'

'You know you are most beautiful woman. We can be good together.'

'We should really get a contract drawn up,' Paul said firmly. 'I'll ask my agent to send you our usual one.'

'Why we needing contract and agent? We do between us. Cut out the middleman.' He produced the phrase with a flourish like the magician's rabbit.

'I'm afraid that's not possible. I have my contract with my own gallery which I always stick to.'

'I can give you much more. I give you work best publicity. I give you share of sales.'

'Yes, the 2% resale right fee.'

'No, no. More, much more. 50%. I charge much and they pay because Kravic says is worth it. So we work together. I like work with beautiful woman.'

'Look Mr Kravic, you've been good or I might say, perceptive enough to buy my work. Not me. What you do with it is your business, literally, and I can have no further interest in it except for my legally due 2%.' Paul swallowed her coffee and stood up.

'Please not to be angry although it is very fine.' For a moment Paul thought he was about to throw his arms around her and imprison her. Then he stepped back. 'I will wait. I will send you money all same.'

Paul put down her cup and moved carefully towards the door. 'Wait. I open.' Kravic seized her hand and kissed it. Then with a bow he opened the door and let her pass through. Turning sharply right she almost ran along the corridor to the next turn. Then she paused and leant against the wall, her heart thudding, hoping she wasn't going to faint. 'This was how that poor bloody N Y chambermaid must have felt,' she thought, 'only she didn't get off so lightly.'

❧ ❧ ❧

'How did it go then?'

'Don't ask?'

'It's what you always ask me.'

'If I still had my virginity I'd say I just about escaped with it intact.'

Putting aside her papers Terry got up from her chair and put her arms round Paul. 'So it wasn't just your etchings he was after.'

'Aren't you jealous?'

'Of course. Wildly.'

'That's alright then. Wasn't it called 'the casting couch' in the great days of Hollywood?'

'He didn't suspect you were gay?'

'That would have turned him on even more: 'What you need is a real man;' That sort of crap.'

'Poor baby. Give me a kiss.'

'That's better. Another one. Now tell me how yours went.'

'Grim. Bill Stiles says we have to be prepared for another 'yes' vote and what that would mean.'

'That's no way to go into a campaign.'

'He's being realistic. They've contacted all the Scottish constituencies for their sense of it all and the results are pretty negative. We've let people down is the feeling. Relied on their loyalty without really listening. They're just drifting away. 'Let's give it a try,' that sort of thing. You know that very British reaction: 'Let the others have a go and see what they can do.' The trouble is this is different. There's no way back if it doesn't work. Bill says we should start considering our own futures.'

'As bad as that!'

'I wondered: would you come up for a few days, take in Glasgow on the way; see what chance Prof Jane thinks I have of getting a job up there? You could take some pictures; do some sketching…'

'And get the smell and taste of Kiril Kravic off my hair and out of my mouth. Let's do that.'

⚜ ⚜ ⚜

AD 600

Although King Bruide had received Colm with favour seeing his power from the Lord and had confirmed us in the possession of Hy and given him leave to go among the King's subjects baptising them and building chapels to serve them with such of our company who were called to that work in that place, yet he still kept by him a certain magus, a Briton called Brochan whom he loved because he had been his tutor. This Brochan was angered and jealous at Colm's coming there and whenever he visited King Bruide he would put the holy man to some test saying:

'When O Colm do you propose to set sail?'

To which Colm replied, 'I shall set sail after three days'

'That you shall not,' the magus replied, 'for I shall raise up a wind to blow against you so that your boat can make no progress down Loch Ness.'

'Nevertheless,' said Colm, 'I shall go.'

Then on the appointed morning it was as the magus had foretold that the wind blew from West to East so fiercely that those who had gathered to see Colm set sail feared that the curragh would be driven back or overturned, and the whole earth was covered by a great darkness. Still Colm embarked on his fragile ship and ordered the trembling sailors to hoist the sails against the wind. As soon as the sails were set the ship began to tack fast against the wind so that the many people who had gathered to see him go were full of amazement, and were more so when the wind, as if at his bidding, turned around to speed him along the loch so that he reached his destination that very evening.

And this was the ingratitude and malice of the magus Brochan even after Colm had saved his life. For it happened before this that Colm had pleaded with the magus for the release of a young Irish Scot whom he held captive which, he refusing, the holy man said: 'Know this O Brochan, know that if you refuse to set this woman free you will die before I return to this province.' When he had said this in the presence of King Bruide and his followers then he set out for the river Ness and taking a white pebble from it said to those with him: 'God will make this white pebble able to cure many diseases. At this very moment Brochan is being punished severely, for the glass cup from which he was about to drink has broken in his hand wounding him so that he lies half dead. We will wait here for messengers from the king, begging us to return and help the dying man who has now agreed to free his captive.'

Even as he spoke two horsemen arrived from the king who told all that had happened as Colm had predicted, and that the king and his councillors asked him to return and cure his dying foster-father. Then Colm sent two of his companions to the King saying that if Brochan first promised to free his captive then the pebble should be put in a goblet of water for Brochan to drink. But that if he refused to free his captive he would instantly die.

When the two messengers told all this to the king and the magus they were filled with such fright that they instantly released the captive girl. Then the pebble was put into the cup where it floated like a nut or an apple and Brochan drank of it and was cured at once.

Afterwards the stone was kept among the king's treasures and cured many diseases. But if the sufferer's time to die had come then the stone could not be found. And so it was on the day of King Bruide's death that although they searched high and low, and in the place where it was usually kept, the white pebble was not to be found.

✤ ✤ ✤

201?

They had driven up from London, sharing the driving and stopping for the night in Stockport. Dropping Terry in Glasgow, Paul had driven on alone to the cottage finding the big iron key still safely under the stone that served as a doorstep where terry had left it. Now she waited for a message before going out to shop for their supper. Back again she began on the spaghetti sauce of mushrooms, onions, garlic, herbs and tomato with a dash of red wine. Then she filled the big pan with water for the pasta and went back into the sitting room where she could see when Terry passed the window and hurry to open the door.

'How did it go? What did she say?'

'Give me a hug and let me get in first.' Looking round Terry said, 'You've unpacked the car. You should have waited for me to help.'

'Are you hungry? The pasta will only take a few minutes?'

'Let's have a drink first.'

Paul fetched the bottle, opened it and poured two glasses of Pinot Grigio. 'So, what did your Prof Jane have to offer?'

'She thinks I can get something there, that's my best bet and she's going to see whether there might be a visiting lectureship available. Though she did say that if I was looking for a quiet life academe wasn't the place and it was probably just as cut-throat as Westminster. She says I can combine politics with history which will give me the edge. She also said you should sound out Glasgow S.o.A. for some part-time teaching and try to get some sort of exhibition going here.'

'Good thinking. I'll take my portfolio round to that little gallery in John Street tomorrow.'

'Is all this okay for you? I worry I'm messing up your life. And what about the flat?'

'Well, we shan't be cutting ourselves off completely. We'll need to be in London quite a bit, at least I will, and if things get too tough I can let it. I was thinking I'll need a studio here. The cottage is too small and dark to work in. I'll see if that gallery has any ideas and if not we can put up something in the garden. It's big enough for a decent sized shed. Now I'm going to get on with supper. The sauce is all ready.'

Paul stood up to go out into the small kitchen. Suddenly she felt Terry's arms around her.

'Paul, I'm frightened. You're being so good and calm but I'm terrified of what might happen, to us I mean, in case it's all too much and breaks us up.'

'It hasn't happened yet. We mustn't assume it's going to. It may not go through; it might be a 'no'. People don't always think things through.'

'That's what I'm afraid of.'

'But anyway it can't split us up. Only we can do that.'

⚜ ⚜ ⚜

Part Two

201?

The Joint Committee for Finance, the JCF, is meeting in Berwick-on-Tweed.

'You can't expect to keep sterling as your currency. We suggest you join the Eurozone.' The British Treasury Secretary says.

'On the contrary, and in the present continuing uncertainty we see no reason to change.'

'But you can't stay in sterling if you're out of the Union.'

'I'm afraid we don't accept that. It's our currency too, if we choose it. The Royal Scottish Mint was here in Edinburgh and our banknotes are still currency.'

'Unless we refuse to recognise them.'

'Then you would have to refuse to recognise those of the other British regions which would bring a hornets' nest about your ears.'

'We could make Scotland a special case as the only one that's repudiated the Union.'

'Then we will nationalise the Royal Bank of Scotland and continue to issue our own currency. And there's the Clydesdale. You'd find it hard to starve us out financially with all their investments and branches. And then there's the diaspora. It wouldn't go down too well in the States or with the rest of the Commonwealth. We're still members after all.'

'But RBS belongs to the UK taxpayer.'

'Exactly. And 5 million of them are Scots. As a sovereign nation we can nationalise who we like.'

'And what will you back this up with?'

'An improving economy. England has run us down for years. Now we have ship-building again on the Clyde, wind farms selling you electricity, Norwegian gas and our tourism: our theatres, the festival, support for the arts like the Highland Games that brings in the visitors.'

'You're selling Scotland?'

'Aye. As you sell the Changing of the Guard. And we mean to open up the underpopulated parts of the country to new agriculture, new businesses. We have a skilled workforce with a long tradition in engineering, technology, science, medicine. We shall offer incentives to people to come and expand our economy, grow our cities.'

'You could have done all that within the United Kingdom.'

'When you denied us the third option you took that possibility away.'

'Oh well if you're going to dig up the past and claim it's all our responsibility...' He shuts his folder with a slap, stands and followed by his trio of civil servants goes out into the corridor. 'Bloody women. I hate trying to negotiate with clever arsed women. I suppose she's got a degree in economics.'

'A PhD I think, from Harvard,' one of the aides supplied.

❧ ❧ ❧

AD 600

As I have told you on his first visit to King Bruide in his fortress above the river Ness the King gave Colm leave to preach to his people throughout his Kingdom and to set down cilles as in our own country where the people may be taught and worship Christ. And so first when we had returned to Hy we went North from there into the lands of the Picts beyond Dal Riata, beginning at Mull itself, then Hinba, Tiree and Skye. All these Colm visited in person while many came to us from Scotia for the sake of learning and the love of God, either to join us on Hy or to seek the solitary life as hermits so that there were always labourers in the field.

Some indeed not content even with this, but looking to follow the example of the desert fathers set out to find deserts in the ocean but found instead rocky cliffs haunted by seabirds along the western coast among the islands and the mouths of the great lochs in those parts. These were very treacherous waters and Colm warned us to hug the islands and not commit our boats to the open sea so that the furthest settlement was made at Lewis on the Western side. The land here is one of marsh and mountain and the people themselves are sparse.

So then Colm went again to the king's fortress of Craig Phaedrick to begin his work among the people of the East who, because of the greater fertility of the land for the growing of oats and barley and the grazing of animals, are more numerous. Then from the fortress we could travel both South and North, always returning to the king's dun which lay between them. And although the king had wished to banish all the magi from his court when he first saw Colm's power from God yet they lingered and when we went beyond the walls to sing our evening hymn they tried their best to prevent God's praises being sung among a pagan people. Them Colm began in his great voice to sing psalm 45: 'Eructavit cor meum,' so loudly that the king and all his people inside were filled with terror.

Yet another time when Colm was visiting King Bruide, perceiving through the power of the Spirit that Cormac, who had set out to find a desert in the sea as the latest of those on such a quest, was after some months to be driven ashore on Orkney, Colm asked of the King to command the chief of Orkney who was then on a visit and whose hostages were held by King Bruide, to protect Cormac and his companions, ensuring that no evil was done to them. And all this happened as he had foreseen and they returned safely to Hy.

⚜ ⚜ ⚜

201?

'You okay?'
    'Yeah, you?'
    'Miss you.'
    'Miss you too.'
    'Listen you'll have to get a Visa. They've set up these daft border patrols now. You'll have to bring your passport too. Since England came out of the EU. Thank God for Ireland packing the vote to keep Scotland in once England was out.
    'Will that happen here do you think?'
    ' What visas and stuff? I suppose so. Tit for tat, like kids in the playground.'
    'Where do I get this visa?'
    'Scottish Embassy?'
    'I'll try and sort it out tomorrow.'

'You'll be here for the inaugural?'

'Darling, of course. I'll go round there tomorrow and sit there till they give me one.'

'And why do you need this? What is the purpose of your visit?' The official pushed his glasses up on his nose.

'I have an exhibition opening in the town.'

'You are an artist Ms Sanderson. Scotland is famous for its artists.'

'Elizabeth Blackadder is a fine artist.'

'And will you want to settle in Scotland Ms Sanderson? We are of course much more open than England to immigrants.'

'I have a part time visiting lectureship at the Glasgow School of Art.'

'In that case I have no choice but to stamp your visa. Welcome to Alba, Fàilte!' Paul found herself stretching out her hand to shake his proffered fist, noticing the back of it was darkened by black hairs that grew as far as the roots of his fingers. 'Leonardo would have had fun with that,' she thought and took the slim booklet in saltire blue that he pushed towards her across the table.

The room had a makeshift feel as if it had been hastily assembled from a shop for second-hand office furniture. Soon, she thought, there would be officials behind glassed grills, all the paraphernalia of bureaucracy. 'That's how we try to define who we are, with an official stamp,' she thought, angered and depressed by the whole ritual. She wanted to tear out the pages in their pretty blue cover, rip them apart into a reverse confetti of rejection, or laugh out loud at the absurdity of it all, except that then they would judge her to be 'not a fit person' and take away the newly minted passbook. Could they really stop her at the border and refuse to let her in? As she turned towards the door she had a sudden fantasy of crossing the Cheviots on foot by night like the Von Trapp family in the movie, guided by Queen Victoria's gillie John Brown, played by Sean Connery.

Terry was waiting with the car at Glasgow Station.

'It's so good to see you. How was London?'

'Well I have to say Gallery Kravic have done a great job with setting up the retrospective. Funnily enough my little job at GSA has helped. He's impressed by success, part of the cult of celebrity everywhere I suppose. So I've taken on the mantle of the Scottish colourists and Charles Rennie Mackintosh because he's heard of them.'

'And is he still trying to get into your knickers?'

'No, thank god. I've sort of gone beyond his reach with all this. He now sees himself as my Svengali.'

'He'll be back.'

Soon they were on the ferry crossing the narrow strait to Dunoon. Today the water was grey and freckled with small white-quiffed waves, a texture Paul stored away for later use.

'How's uni?'

'The politics seminars are a bit thorny. The students are so defensive of all things Scots. I'm not at all sure how my inaugural will go down but I have to lay out what I see as the truth.'

'Which is?'

'Unintended consequences, though maybe some people always intended them. I'm so glad you're going to be there to pick up the pieces and glue them together afterwards. By the way you mustn't call it an inaugural; that's my little joke. You only get one of those when you're made up to full professor with a chair and all that. This is just an introductory lecture they've been kind enough to let me give. Something to do with the Prof I imagine.

Paul was glad to see a steady river of students queuing to pass through the single door into the lecture theatre. She had been introduced to the young post-graduate deputed to look after her while Terry was whisked away by Jane Sims. Inside her guide indicated a front row of reserved seats.

'I think I'd rather be further back,' Paul said. 'There's nothing worse than catching someone's eye while they're speaking.' She began to climb up towards the back of the raked lecture theatre, surrounded by a sea of voices, until she found an aisle seat free half way up.

Suddenly the buzz fell silent. Jane Sims was leading Terry in. A couple of stragglers pushed their way through the door. Professor Jane Sims stepped forward to begin her introduction.

'...bringing not just a distinguished academic presence but a hands on knowledge of politics...to speak this morning on the Politics of History, under the title: 'What's in a name?'

Paul heard Terry say 'Good morning everyone. Thank you for giving me this opportunity...' and then her concentration began the process of waxing and waning that often accompanies following someone we know or love performing in public, distanced from us by space, and fear for them, exposed, exposing themselves, even in a friendly medium. And this, she sensed, might not be. She heard Terry say: 'I feel I should perhaps apologize for giving you such a cliché for a title and an English one at that, though we could argue that that particular coining of aperçu or cliché is our most successful global product or perhaps not even ours anymore. But I wanted to consider the names we give ourselves in these islands by considering those we have been given by others in the past and how they have been used by us and others.

Romeo is of course wrong. He's trying to convince himself. Because there is everything in a name. And I shall begin with 731, with Bede and the names he gives us, based on his knowledge of Latin writers, for the inhabitants of these islands, as he says 'at the present time' which are 'the English, the Britons, the Picts and the Scots' by whom of course he means the Irish.'

Paul heard an intake of communal breath and then a murmur she couldn't decipher as either positive or negative. She found she had clenched her hands and deliberately relaxed them. Terry was going on: 'You will notice he uses the term 'Anglii' for all the English Teutonic tribes, perhaps because his own Northumbria was settled by the Angles. We have been stuck with it ever since though the people from the rest of Europe do refer to the Anglo Saxons in a pejorative sense.' Laughter now from the audience.

'Those now known as the Welsh, a term for foreigner put on them by the English after Bede's time, he calls the Britons which would include not only the Cymri but the Britons of the Cornish Peninsula and Strathclyde, now the Lake District, Cumberland and Westmoreland but, until recently before then, stretching Northwards to here and further on to Loch Lomond with its capital at Dumbarton. So where we are sitting now was neither Scotland nor Alba but Alt Clut and after 870 ,Strathclyde, a Brythonic-speaking kingdom, also known as Cumbria. To return to Bede, he separates out the Picts, giving them a history worthy of a Hollywood blockbuster, as wandering Scythians who first tried to settle in Ireland and, when they were refused, were advised by the natives to try Britain where they colonised the North of the island. Bede doesn't seem to know about the Cruithneana or Irish Picts mentioned by earlier writers such as Adomnan some 30 years before. Perhaps history had already deleted them or the Irish were unwilling to admit their perseverance. Rather what we try to do with those who don't fit: Travellers, Roma, gippos as they used to be called by my mother and her neighbours.

Which brings me to his last group, the Scotti, from Scotia, sometimes called Hibernia, the Irish, immigrants as the English were in Britain, and indeed everyone else who has ever colonised these islands since the last ice age receded making the land habitable again. Not until the late Middle Ages did the mess of potage of names, tribes, and kingdoms settle into the four regions, absorbing the Norse invaders and the relocated Northmen of Norway and Britons of Brittany along the way.

What do we do when we name people, places, concepts? We create myths: names are part of myth. Politics is rife with it. Take the names of parties at Westminster. Labour for those who have never laboured, including the unemployed; Conservatives who abolished planning laws which can preserve the environment; Lib Dems who subscribe to a concept of Liberalism that harks back to free markets not social, sexual or cultural liberation. And then there are the nano-tribes of caste and class. But here I want to ask you to examine local myths. Scotland today, like England, is a composite of Picts, Britons, Irish and Norse settlers from Scandinavia; a mongrel construct in fact.'

Paul heard an angry murmur rising around her. Some of the audience stamped their feet but Terry went on:

'That isn't my area of concern in this lecture. My suggestion here today is that we examine for ourselves all the myths we have created with our naming, and what we are trying to do with them, what we are hiding, and where they might lead. Suppose for example we renamed Glasgow and surrounds, Strathclyde, Alt Clut, and separated it from the

Highlands and Islands. And how would Edinburgh react to moving the capital to Dumbarton?'

Laughter this time: 'You see. Tribes can be created and recreated: Rangers against Celtic, Edinburgh versus Glasgow? Tribalism is our legacy and the source of so many of our myths, of our wars although a recent book attempts to make it the source of our success as dominant animal species on the planet. And we don't need to look far east to Shia against Sunni; we have our own home breed: Prod against Mick. You can fill in the rest.

The first both Muslim; the second both Christian. And both against each other, as we see tragically everyday.

Those who study the history of politics know, or should know, this. The past looked at through microscope and telescope should show us the present and what we could do with it. "Today we have naming of parts," and those parts are those of an island, a continent, a world, and all the myths we attach to the names. That line is part of a World War II poem. The parts are those of a weapon of war, rifle or machine gun. The meaning is meant to desensitize the recruits and normalize an object that will be used to kill. The exercise fails because the recruit's mind wanders, playing over the nearby gardens with their on-going natural life of blossom and bees, cancelling out the naming of parts. Politics uses history often spuriously to encourage the myth making inherent in names but we must always be prepared to let our minds and our aspirations wander beyond the names that might limit our horizons. In politics there is everything in a name. But Romeo and Juliet both ended up dead. That was the background. Now for the political detail...

There was a moment's silence when the lecture ended. Then a mingled cacophony of boos and cheers.

Some were on their feet clapping vigorously while others sat fast and slow hand-clapped. Jane Sims stepped up to the lectern as Terry took her seat.

'Well, Dr Ellis has certainly started a debate that I suspect will run and run. May I have the customary round of applause for our speaker please.' She turned towards Terry and began to clap. Others joined in while some sat with ostentatiously stilled hands. Jane Sims led the way off the platform and out through a side door on the opposite side of that used by the audience who were queuing to get through.

Paul stood up, making her way along the row and out onto the stepped central aisle. There was a reception for invited guests. Behind her she heard someone say: 'A lot of sound bites; not much substance,' and guessed from the timbre of the voice it was one of the staff. 'Well,' the voice went on, 'we might as well have a free glass of wine at the department's expense.'

A woman's voice said: 'Where did she come from?'

'Ex MP. One of Jane's protégées.'

At the foot of the aisle Paul stood back to let the couple pass. Unsure of the layout of the building or where the reception might be she decided to follow them. There was no sign of Terry spirited away to press the flesh by Jane. For a moment Paul longed to be back in her London eyrie, away from this alien atmosphere, to be safe in her studio, brush in hand or just dreaming, letting her unconscious skills dictate the next stroke. Then she followed her unknowing guides along a corridor and turned into a room full of light and voices vying with each other. Students flanked either side of the door with trays of drinks. Hoping it wasn't warm, Paul helped herself to a glass of pallid white wine, and began peering about for

Terry, finally tracking her down in the middle of a small group, firmly chaperoned by Jane.

Moving over to the little cluster she kissed Terry: 'Well done. You were great.'

'Jane, you remember Paul,' Terry said.

'Yes of course. So glad you could come.' Paul found herself embraced.

'You must come over to Dunoon and see Paul's exhibition there.'

'I'd love to. There's the Head of School. I must go and have a word.'

'When can we leave?'

'Not quite yet but people will drift away quite soon. Was it really okay?'

'I said you were great. You really got them going, thinking.' Paul saw the couple she had overheard earlier approaching. 'Watch out for this guy,' she murmured.

'Professor McBride. How good of you to come. I won't ask if you approved of my talk.' Terry laughed. 'More politics than history. I'm afraid I've been corrupted by Westminster. Can I introduce Paula Sanderson.'

'Do you live locally Ms Sanderson,' McBride asked when they had shaken hands all round.

'I'm up for the opening of a little exhibition of my work.'

'You're an artist?'

'That's for others to decide,' Paul laughed, defusing question and answer. 'I just do the stuff.'

'Are you of the Eminite or the Hirstian school?'

'Well I rather hope it's the Sandersonian.'

'I want to introduce you to Jay Wills, she's medieval art, over there. Will you excuse us.' Terry began to move Paul away. As they went she heard McBride saying: 'I suppose they're, what is it, an item?'

'Oh do you think so.'

'Who was the woman? She hardly said a word.'

'That's the McBride speciality: silencing people, especially female colleagues. So I don't really know but I think she's the industrial revolution.'

'If I'd have known that I'd have asked her about the matchgirls' strike. That would really have upset him.'

'You're so untazed by all this. It makes me want to kiss you.'

'That would cheer up McBride.'

'Here's Jay. Jay this is Paula Sanderson, who's up for the opening of her show.'

'Where is it? I must drop by and see it.'

'I'm afraid it's over the water,' Paul said, 'not in the city.'

'That's okay.'

'Let us know when you're coming and come for a drink. You haven't seen the cottage.'

'Great. I'll email you.'

'Come soon before Paul has to go back to London.'

'Yes do! In fact come to the opening on Friday if you can.'

'Well that took the taste of McBride away,' Paul said when they were on their way home. 'You needed one friendly face other than Jane's. But not too friendly eh?'

'Idiot! Dear idiot! I've invited some of my old local party lot to the opening. Is that okay? They haven't got much money so I don't suppose they'll buy anything but they'll swell the numbers. And Jim is bringing someone from the local rag.'

'I've put in some prints from sketches I've done locally and they're quite cheap. Somebody might want one of those.'

'I don't want you to be disappointed.'

'I shan't be. I'll just be glad if anyone turns up, and a mention in the local paper would be really cool. It'll look good with the school; maybe encourage them to buy something.'

❧ ❧ ❧

Terry didn't know which of them was more nervous as they waited for the first to arrive. The gallery owner Harry Townley was philosophical. 'They'll be here. Don't you worry.' Another in-comer, he wore baggy tweeds that looked as if they were just back from a day's shooting, and a deer stalker with the ear flaps down in dangling, greenish brown sideboards, old leather sandals over woolly socks. 'The perfect English gent,' Paul had called him.

The first customers were two women of Harry's vintage who kept a small petshop, barely surviving in competition with the supermarket.' 'These are really very nice. I was afraid they'd be just…you know…modern.'

Harry Townley had installed himself behind the bar table.

'A glass of wine, ladies, on the house.'

'Look Elizabeth isn't that our bothy? Oh we must have it. Mr Townley who do we speak to buy one?'

'You speak to me. Are you sure you can afford it? You can pay in instalments if that would help.'

'Oh we mustn't lose it.'

'Right, if you're sure I'll put a red sticker on it; the first.'

'Please Mr Townley. Look at that Jessie. It's ours and we're the first.'

'There's Jim with some of the old committee,' Terry was waving towards the door where more people were arriving.

'Evening Laird,' A tall stocky man was taking a glass from Harry Townley.

'Jim, good of you to come. You remember Paula.'

'Of course; congratulations.'

'Why did you call Harry, 'Laird', was it?'

'Because he is. He inherited the title and what was left of the estate from an uncle or cousin. Something like that, and decided to settle here. He could probably, technically, raise the militia or something. The Townleys were absentee landlords, up for the shooting that sort of set up. Kept themselves to themselves and their London guests. Harry's not like that. The Laird bit is a joke between us.' He turned to Paul. 'Any difficulty getting through our new border controls?'

'Terry had warned me so I'd got my passport and visa at the ready.'

'Didn't it make you angry?'

'It made me sad that the first thing we do is put up barriers against each other.'

'I hear they're displaying troops along the border and at all parts now the Assembly's taken over the old Highlanders, and split it up into the even older ones like the Black Watch, the Gordons, Argyll and Sutherland, Borderers and so on,' someone said.

'Don't they owe allegiance to the crown?'

'Oh the queen's still queen of Scotland.'

'An English queen?'

'Well she's half Scot through her mother, Lady Elizabeth Bowes Lyon, brought up at Glamis Castle; Bowes had the money, Lyon had the title. Or was it the other way round? Anyway according to old Pictish laws of descent it was through the mother so that makes the Queen legit,' Terry said.

'And after her?'

'Oh Anne of course. She could be crowned at Scone. '

'Or Dunkeld if you want to go back to Kenneth McAlpin! Or even Iona.'

'Seriously Terry,' Jim said, 'you ought to be in there somewhere with all your know -how of how it all works.'

'It's all a bit Alice in Wonderland for me Jim. I'd rather stick to history for now. It's more restful.'

'Well I hope we're going to see you at meetings and maybe on the committee. We need your expertise.'

'What will Scotland do for ships and aircraft, with only soldiers?'

'Start building on the Clyde again for one.'

'I think Paula should circulate,' Terry said, 'and I need another drink. See you later everybody.'

'Will they mind you going off like that?' Paul said. 'I don't want them to resent me.'

'Jim knows me. He'll understand I'd had enough. Come on. You've got your public to attend to. Look there's several more red stickers now.'

'It's going just fine,' Harry Townley said as he poured them fresh glasses. 'You did right to price some of the prints within local pockets.'

'I hope Jay Wills turns up,' Terry said, 'she said she was coming.'

Jim was approaching with a middle-aged man in tow. 'This is Ewan Henessy from the Echo, our revered broadsheet. He'd like a wee word.'

'Shall we go next door, where it's quieter,' Paul said. 'Have you had a chance to look at the pictures?'

Terry turned away, searching the room which was now nicely full. Jay Wills was standing in a far corner studying the picture in front of her.

'Jay, so glad you could come.'

'I really like this. She's very clever.'

The picture was one of Paul's more difficult compositions, some would have said. Across a shadowy landscape other figures picked their way: strange beasts, upright on their flanks, twining serpents, lettering in an old script while the borders were fringed with a pattern of soft verticals, above and below a horizontal line.

'It says: "I love you," Jay said, 'and so do the borders.'

'I know.' Terry was smiling, 'And it's not for sale.'

❧ ❧ ❧

'I felt I should see you myself rather than leave it to the Dean,' The Principal carefully replaced a stray pencil in the folder on his desk.' We have had a number of complaints following your lecture the other night. In fact I might say you've stirred up quite a hornets' nest. Things have changed somewhat since you were a student here, which was before my time of course. Students no longer sit at our feet taking in what we have to offer them, even though here they are not quite customers in the English sense. There is the greatest support for an independent state among young people looking for change, which is why the then First Minister was so eager to have them included in the ballot, though personally I thought sixteen was too young. Our eighteen year olds are easily influenced enough by romantic ideas. You made your position quite clear and I have to ask was that wise?'

'Well I'm sorry, of course, to have caused you and the college any unpleasantness. I thought I was merely pointing out what seems to me a misunderstanding, leading to a misuse of historical myth.' Terry said.

'Others don't see it as myth of course. That is your problem.'

'That's why it seemed worth pointing out. To make people think about the concepts that inform politics and then get translated into action, often with unforeseen consequences.'

'Nevertheless that is the situation we have, and you are now part of. It would be unfortunate if many students refused to attend your courses or if the press were to get hold of that. We are after all a largely government funded body. So I must ask you to present your personal underpinning in a more balanced way.'

'You mean water it down?'

'It is, after all, only your theoretical approach, as is so much in the humanities. At least with science you can show results to back up the theory.'

'My hope is that we won't see any results to back up my theory.'

'I also have to remind you that your contract is only for the first year subject to renewal. I don't want to emphasize that, just to make sure you fully understand the position in these changed times.'

'Thank you Principal. I think I do understand better now. I realise I was perhaps rather living in the past, a fault with historians.'

'It's a matter of presentation. I'm sure you can work something out. I know Professor Sims thinks very highly of you.'

'I felt so feeble, so wet,' Terry said afterwards. 'Just sitting there and taking it but I don't want to lose this job, not yet. I suppose that's how corruption begins: on one side with power and on the other with fear.'

'You're the least corruptible person I know,' Paul said. 'That's why you spoke up for what you believed in your lecture.'

'And now I've blown it by being weak.'

'You haven't blown it. You've just had a chunk of reality thrown at you.'

'I wish you were here.'

'So do I.'

'At least there's only a couple of weeks to the end of term.'

✤ ✤ ✤

AD 600

At another time when Colm was travelling in Pictland a man from a local family hearing him preach the word of God through an interpreter was converted and husband, wife and children and all his household was baptized. It so happened that a few days later one of the man's sons was struck by a violent pain so that he was close to death, in danger of losing his life.

When the pagan magi saw that he was dying they began to blame the parents and laugh at them, praising their own gods and saying that they were the strong ones, and pouring scorn on Christ as weaker than them. When Colm heard all this and that God was mocked, he rose up and accompanied by his companions, he went to the place where the local family were preparing to celebrate the funeral rites for the dead boy. Seeing their great grief he comforted them, and told them not to doubt the power of the Lord. Then he asked, 'In which house is the body of the dead child?'

Then the father led Colm to that sad place, and leaving everyone else outside, Colm went in alone and fell on his knees beside the child, calling aloud to Christ our Lord with tears pouring down his face which fell upon the dead child's eyelids, and at the sound of his voice the eyes were opened. Then Colm cried out, 'In the name of Our Lord Jesus Christ rise up and stand upon your feet.' And when his voice had restored life to the body and the eyes were reopened Colm took the boy by the hand, and steadying him on his feet, led him out of the building and restored him to his parents. Then grief was changed to joy and all the people gathered around glorified Jesus Christ with a great shout.

Yet another time when he was travelling beyond Druim Alban, which are the mountains that separate Pictland from our Dal Riata, for he went often to preach to the different people as it says in the poem:

From the Ietian Sea, the Gaels,

Cruithneans, Saxons, Brito Sax, greatest among men

Was the man who went to preach

For thirty years living among them.

While as I say he had passed over the backbone of Britain one of his companions, a young monk, Fintan the son of Aedh was struck with a great sickness which greatly grieved his friends who begged Colm to pray for him. Moved by their suffering, Colm stretched out his hands towards heaven, and blessing the sick boy said: 'This young man for whom you have interceded will live a long life and after we have all gone he will remain and die of a ripe old age.'

Then Fintan recovered and is yet living, while as he foretold, Colm himself is gone, and many of the brothers at the monastery that he has founded on the wild coast of Morvern. And I would add that through the goodness of

God wherever Colm has journeyed has remained free of the sickness, as I believe though some say it is the sweetness of the air and others that it cannot cross Druim Alban. Thanks be to God.

❧ ❧ ❧

201?

Paul is driving South down the M74. She hasn't come this way by car for a few months. Yesterday they took down the last of the little exhibition which has been running all this time by local request, and loaded the unsold pictures together with other work she's been doing, into their old estate car. This morning she set off, aiming to stop at Manchester to break the journey.

'No dancing in Piccadilly,' Terry had said. 'No clubbing.'

'It's okay, I'll be too tired.'

She's nearly at Carlisle now, junction 44 where she can stop for a pee and a sandwich and coffee before the second lap. Suddenly there seems to be a jam ahead, traffic blocking all the lanes and only inching forward. At first she can't see what's causing it. Then as she too moves up the queue she can make out a gantry across the road, high up, with the words 'You Are Now Leaving Scotland,' picked out in blue on a white ground with the Gaelic version beside them.

She hadn't reckoned on this, that there would be border controls on the motorway. Whose fault is it: Scotland, Alban or England, Britain? At last she reaches the row of gated booths. A notice says: Immigration and Customs. Anything to Declare? She winds down the window and proffers her passport to the figure leaning out of the glass and metal booth. He takes her passport and then: 'What's in the back of the vehicle?'

'Just my work.'

'Your work?'

'Yes.'

'And what would that be?'

'I'm an artist.' Paul always feels self-conscious applying the word to herself although it's only a factual expression of what she does.

'I'll have to ask you to drive into that bay,' he is pointing, 'and switch off your engine please miss.'

Paul hasn't taken in that each booth has a filter lane on the far side ending in another gate. She moves into it and switches off as she's been told. The officer has come out of the booth and steps up to her window.

'Is the rear door locked?'

'No, it's open.'

He goes round to the back, clicks on the lock and raises the tailgate. Paul can hear him fossicking about among her work, he comes back to her window.

'You say these are yours?'

'Yes.'

'Can you prove that miss? Documentation?'

'Look, I'll show you.' Paul gets out of the car and leads the official round the back again. 'You've got my passport there. The pictures are all signed. Check the name.'

He begins to painstakingly lean each one forward as they are racked, glancing from the passport to Paul's signature scrawled on the backs.

'Shouldn't it be on the painting itself; usually bottom right hand corner?'

'I prefer it on the back, and for purposes of establishing ownership it doesn't matter where it is as long as it's there.'

'Is that so. Well you'll need an export licence to take possibly valuable works of art out of the country. I take it these are for sale?'

'I hope so. Do I need an export licence for my own work accompanied by me?'

'All goods, including works of art. Don't worry. It isn't hard. You can still sit here and fill it in, or go over to the office there.' He is pointing to a low pre-fab building to one side. 'You'll need to estimate the value. Works of art over a certain value are subject to a restraining order that allows the National Gallery of Scotland the right to bid for them. The system's only just up and running so we're not being too tough until people get used to it.'

'And what happens if I want to bring some of them back?'

'You'll need an import licence. I'll just get you that form. We have to be careful you see; they could be stolen goods.'

'Do I look like that sort of person?'

'You'd be surprised. They come in all shapes and sizes and what better cover for a mule than a handsome lassie.'

Paul wonders if she should curtsey and say: 'Thank you kind sir,' Instead she sits quietly in the driving seat waiting for the promised form, drained, part frightened, part angered by the whole episode.

❧ ❧ ❧

Jim McCullan had called in for a drink. 'It would be good to catch up,' he'd said in his text message inviting himself, 'and nobody's to even mention Auld Lang Syne.'

'I wouldn't dream of it,' Terry had texted back. 'It would be good to see you too. You still a Glenfiddich fan?'

The end of the academic year was beckoning. She and Paul were taking a friend's cottage on Skiathos. Since her interview with the Principal Terry had concentrated more on history in her lectures, less on its entwinement in politics.

'How's it going at Uni?' Jim asked when they were settled with glasses in their hands.

Terry wrinkled her nose as at a bad smell. 'I got a ticking off for making my views on tribalism too explicit so I've been keeping my head down. There were complaints apparently.'

'Who from?'

'I was given to understand from students.'

'Wet behind the ears! What do they know?'

'Oh I can understand it. They're young; they want change, they want hope. It's a form of idealism.'

'What happened to the old idealisms?'

'They were killed off by consumerism, late capitalism.'

'You don't believe that.'

'I do and I don't. It's made the world a greyer, more homogenized place. Some of this is a hankering for colour and excitement. That's why people watch reality competitions. It gives them the illusion that they, anyone, can be a celebrity and that in our society if you're not born into privilege which people think brings not just comfort, enough, but the super charge of change and excitement, you just have to win a contest, be a footballer or a popstar and you've got it made.'

'It's very depressing. I suppose they keep you pretty busy at the Uni?'

'I'll say.'

'You wouldn't have time to do a bit for us again?'

'What did you have in mind?'

'We need good, educated people who can see further than their noses. We've a fight on with the PSA.'

'They're new to me. Who are they?'

'In English: The Alban Freedom Party. Extreme separatists and extremists. Do you remember Anders Breivik back in 2011, gunned down all those kids at a summer camp in Sweden? The PSA are our own version. They particularly resent the landshare policy of giving land to immigrants with the help of EU funding. They're against what they call the Balkanisation of large areas, previously unoccupied but now having an influx of what they call 'peasants', crofters we called them in the Highlands, used to subsistence farming, from Greece, Romania, Bulgaria and so on. Areas that were emptied in the clearances are being farmed again but not by native Scots.'

'And they're gaining support?'

'They won seats in the local elections for the first time. I'd say they're the extreme form of what you've always fought against Terry.'

'You're very flattering, Jim, trying to persuade me but I don't feel ready to get back into that world yet.'

'Maybe later? I'll not give up on you then.'

❧   ❧   ❧

Paul is on her way to the art school where she is giving a series of occasional lectures. Today it's on minimalist sculpture and maquettes, and why she enclosed her recent work in glass boxes, vitrines. She's prepared for someone to ask whether she was influenced by Damien Hirst to do this but she will explain that, once, when she was still a student herself she came across an old catalogue fro an exhibition called Heads and Boxes which featured the polystyrene heads from tailors' dummies one of which had been partly cut away and filled with models of animal grotesques labelled Bosch! And then there were other maquettes inside transparent cases showing an affinity with set designs.

Kravic's interest in her and her work though not without its problems, had brought her an international reputation she hadn't had before. Next week she is off to Mexico City for the opening of a show which includes some of her work. She wishes Terry were going with her but it's term time with no chance of her getting away.

She is walking up towards the art school to stretch her legs after the ferry and bus ride. Turning the corner into Bath Street she suddenly finds the way blocked by a police cordon kettling what seems to be some sort of protest. She only has a few moments to take in the scene before she turns back to find another route but it's enough to see that the protesters, mostly male, are in kilts of a uniform blue, black and white tartan, many of them waving the national flag and with a sprinkling of banners. Paul's eyes flick across the painted slogans: This Land is Ours; Caledonia for Caledonians.

She is forced to take Sauchiehall Street which she had hoped to avoid because of the throng of tourists. Hurrying because the detour has made her late, she makes her way to the staff cloakroom, where she's allowed a locker as merely a visitor, instead of an office. Pugh Evans turns from washing his hands.

'Hi!'

Pugh has been friendly and helpful to her, filling her in on the quaint customs and procedures that grow up in all corporate bodies, and easing her way round the galaxy of buildings and mazy corridors. Himself a distinguished print-maker, he appreciates Paul's work and her dedication to it.

'I'm late,' she says, 'but hi. I got stopped by some demo. A lot of hairy legs in woolly socks and kilts.'

'Blue, black and white tartan?'

Paul nods. 'Yep.'

'That'll be the PSA or the Sons of Wallace. It's an anti-immigration party.'

'You've lost me. I'm not very well up in Scottish politics.'

'The present government wants to increase the population, give us more clout than the five million which isn't even as much as London though it's more than Ireland, that is if you exclude Northern Ireland. They want to reverse the Highland Clearances.'

'Terry would know all about that but I'm afraid I don't.'

'It's a long story of declining then increasing population with the introduction of the potato, then with the Jacobite rising, falling again as thousands left for the States. Then the clearances when aristocratic landlords decided there was more money in sheep than in kelp potash and herrings. The Countess of Sutherland kicked fifteen thousand off her million acres for example. Then came the potato famine. Lots went to Canada, Nova Scotia.'

'Just like Ireland?'

'The same. Though the Irish rather favoured Australia as a bolthole. Anyway there's plenty of unoccupied land and the EU Common Agricultural Policy makes farming parts of it or managing some for wildlife sustainable again. Only our kids want to live in the cities. A farming life in the wilds doesn't attract them. But those guys, the PSA, would rather it was left empty than 'coigrich' should settle on it.'

'That sounds like dog in the manger. I must go. I've got some setting up to do before my lecture.'

'Maybe we could have a drink some time. Where do you stay when you're up?'

'With Terry, my partner. She has a cottage over on the Cowal Peninsula. Must run. See you later.' Paul hopes this has put him off any ideas for future more intimate encounters he might be incubating. Pugh Evans is nice enough and he could be a useful friend with his local knowledge, and she genuinely likes his work. But she doesn't want to be thought to be leading him on, to be a 'cock teaser', a term born out of male frustration with a friendly, attractive, but sexually unavailable woman. She hopes he won't hate or despise her.

⚜ ⚜ ⚜

'Heard the latest?' It's Terry's turn to cook and she turns round, haloed by a cloud of steam with a saucepan lid in her hand, when Paul comes into the cottage kitchen. 'I'm doing tagliatelle. Is that okay?'

'Great. I'll get us a glass. Tell me in a minute.' Paula fetched two glasses and took a bottle of wine from the fridge. Taking one over to the stove she said: 'No kiss?'

'Sorry I was so longing to tell you and not wanting the pasta to overcook. Come here.'

'So what's this earthshaking event that can't wait?'

'The government is going to introduce a bill to make same-sex marriage legal.'

'But we don't believe in marriage!'

'No we don't but others do and if gays want it, from the point of view of equality they should be able to have it, don't you think?'

'I suppose so.'

'And it might make the rest of society more accepting.'

'Then logically they should extend civil partnerships to straights.'

'Won't you get all the 'family values' lobby against you?'

'I think you will anyway. I haven't told you about my little adventure.'

'I'll dish up first before it gets too soft.'

After a few mouthfuls Terry said, 'So what happened.
Go on.'

'This is great!' Paula hesitated with a forkful of pasta on
its way to her mouth. 'Well nothing really happened. I ran
into a demo and had to backtrack along Sauchiehall Street.'

'Where was it?'

'Outside some government building to do with land.
The police had cordoned off the whole street.'

'That'll be the PSA. Were they all in the same tartan?'

'Yes. Are they all the same clan?'

'Anyone can invent a tartan. The clan thing is quite late
along with the rest of it. Like Queen Victoria reinventing all
the trappings of the English monarchy, the street theatre of
royal occasions that we've learnt to put on so effectively as if
it had been around for centuries.'

'Do you think Hitler learned to stage the Nuremburg
rally from that? And Stalin, and Mao?'

'Maybe. But we're better at the fancy dress parade
whereas theirs were all meant to intimidate with the dark
uniforms, the uniformity, the mechanical marching. Ours is
a sort of pantomime to keep the kids happy.'

'Distract them from what's really going on you mean.
The police were taking the demo seriously but it looked a
bit like Gilbert and Sullivan to me.'

A few days later Jane Sims emailed Terry. 'Could you
drop in for a chat?'

It wasn't a request Terry told Paul, it was more a case of
'she who must be obeyed,' put in the nicest way. Jane had
been good in getting her into the university with a glowing
recommendation, but had carefully stood back since Terry

had taken up the post, to avoid any charge of favouritism. Now she wanted to see her. Terry wondered if it had anything to do with her interview with the Principal but that had been some time ago and she had heard nothing more since, and had been careful not to estrange patriotic students with her outspokenly different views.

'Have a pew,' the professor said, after giving Terry a preliminary hug. 'How's it all going?'

'Okay I think.' She paused: 'You heard about my little run in with the Principal?'

'Because of your introductory lecture? He did mention it at the time. It's all this stuff about student satisfaction. We didn't have it in my student days. We just griped among ourselves. Any overt criticism and you were told not to come to those lectures any more. No, that isn't what I wanted to talk about. Have you heard about the government's gay marriage proposals?'

'A bit?'

'What do you think?'

'That people should be able to have it if they want. It doesn't actually harm anyone else. But why?'

'That's a relief. I was afraid you might be actively campaigning for it.'

Terry laughed. 'That's alright then. What do you think will happen? Why are you worried about it?'

'I think they're going to run into a lot of opposition from both the kirk and the Catholics and that others will try to jump on the bandwagon for their own ends.'

'But that shouldn't affect us here surely.'

'I'm afraid it will. You see we have quite active religious societies in the college. Already I've seen posters going up announcing protest meetings.'

'So we're in for a religious war, our own jihad,' Terry said. 'But haven't we got our own GBLT association. Surely they'll have something to say.'

'I'm worried that that will only make it worse. Tear the university apart.'

'Do you think the government shouldn't have raised it then?'

'Of course not. It's just that here in the university we've got problems enough already.'

'Well it's not usual for me to support the government but this seems like one time we should.'

'Except that a lot of people here think differently. Oh not me of course. You know me. But the nature of democracy is that people can make the wrong choice. Think of the end of the Roman Empire. And I wouldn't want your position here to be threatened, if you got drawn in I mean.'

'Don't worry Jane, I'll keep my head down, unless of course I'm asked a direct question. I won't lie. But surely there must be supporters among the students and other staff. It can't just be you and me.'

'Yes of course. But a lot of people won't want to put their heads above the parapet if the going gets really rough. I expect the antis to be much more vocal. Radicalism isn't fashionable among those trying to get into the jobs market.'

'Now you've really depressed me.'

'Do you think they're really all so, so conformist?' Paul asked when Terry told her about the conversation.

'We've got a lot of middle class English students who are here to get their degrees and then get back to London and a foot on the white collar ladder, no doubt with a leg up from daddy. They'll think it's nothing to do with them.'

'Something about 'the best lacking all conviction'?'

'I don't know about 'the best' but if you're thinking of Yeats, certainly 'the worst are full of passionate intensity."

'I wonder what he would have made of gay marriage,' Paul said.

'Terry laughed.' I doubt if it ever crossed his mind.'

'Well Somerville and Ross were around in Ireland. Do you think he read any of their books? After all he was keen on women who rode to hounds.'

'The awful thing about this kind of situation is you start inventing your own form of tribalism. Us and them. 'Gay is Great!"'

⚜ ⚜ ⚜

AD 600

Although St Molaisse had laid on Colm that he should go into exile and not return to Hibernian Scotia until he had converted as many souls to Christ as had been slain in their sins at the battle of Cul Drebne, when he had been many years in Scotia Alba labouring among the Picts and had caused many places of learning and worship to be established among them and among his own kinsmen there and had drawn men of all the nations of Britain and Scotia to our monastery of Hy there came a call that he should return for a great meeting of the kings. This was to be held at the hill of Drum Celt which lies just beyond Derry, between Aed mac Ainmirech, King of the Northern O'Neill and Aedan mac Gabrain, King of Dal Riata in Scotia and Alba, to agree a peace between them. Therefore they called on Colm to give a blessing on their meeting.

Now at this great meeting a boy was brought to Colm to be blessed and, when he asked the foster parents who had brought him, whose son he was they told him he was Domnall the son of the same King Aed. When he had blessed the child Colm said: 'This boy will outlive all his brothers and be a very famous king and he will never fall into the hands of his enemies but will die peacefully in old age in his own house with a great crowd of family and friends around him.'

Colm had many years before been unwilling to ordain Aedan mac Gabrain King of Dal Riata because he favoured his brother Eoganan. But when he was staying on Hinba he saw on three nights running a vision of an angel with a glass book commanding him to ordain Aedan who was waiting for him at Hy. So at last he accepted God's will and crossed to Hy where he laid his hand on Aedan's head and blessed him.

At the same time as the meeting of kings, Colm wished to visit Scanlan the son of Colman, who was held in chains by King Aedh as a hostage and when he had blessed him, Colm comforted him saying: 'My son, do not despair but be happy and take comfort. And the king who has you fettered will leave this world before you, and after some time in exile you will reign among your people for thirty years, and after a few more days of exile your subjects will invite you back and you will reign for a short three years more.'

Yet again as he was on his way back and passing through Coleraine towards the coast, and with him Abbot Comgall, the two sat down to rest on a fine day in summer near to the fort mentioned before. A bronze basin of spring water was brought to them to wash their hands. Then Colm, in taking it, foretold that one day the spring from which the water came would become unfit to drink, and when Comgall asked why, he said that Colm replied that it would be filled with human blood from the great battle that would be fought between the kin of the two of them. And in that battle Domnall mac Aedh, the boy he had blessed at the meeting of the kings, was the victor.

Then they continued on their way through Coleraine to where Bishop Conall had gathered together a great crowd of people to welcome them and had prepared a lodging for the travellers. The people had brought many gifts which were laid out in the open for Colm to see and to bless, which he did, excepting only those whose donors were greedy and avaricious, but singling out those for praise which were offered by a rich man who was generous to the poor.

✤ ✤ ✤

201?

Paul is in Mexico City, courtesy of the British Council, somewhere she had never expected to be. This time the work on show is paintings and prints because the little vitrines are too fragile to risk and anyway the Kravic Gallery now has most of them, in a much larger display room than at first, which has become a theatre of small still scenes or as Paul sometimes thinks, an early mutascope, the act of passing from one silent image to the other like the flick forward to the next picture. She can't decide whether it's sweet-toothing eye-candy or a kind of artistic soft porn. She senses that Kravic himself would be happy with more of the latter.

The gallery is in the Polanco, 'an affluent district' the guidebook calls it, where the streets are named after international writers, philosophers and scientists. She had hoped the gallery would be on Oscar Wilde but instead it's on Dickens. 'At least he's a Brit,' Terry had said.

'It's not like you to be a xenophobe.'

'Oh I'm not against Horace or Moliere or Schiller. And at least it's not the Coampos Eliseos or I might never see you again.'

'I think you'd better give me back that guide book before you get too morbid.'

The upstairs room, light and airy, is crowded for the opening of the contemporary British art exhibition with, mainly, natives of the city but with a few ex-pats sprinkled here and there. Paul isn't sure if they've all come for the art or the excellent and abundant food and drink. The cultural attaché has just made a speech about 'show-casing Britain through its creative industries.' Suddenly Paul feels very alone, wishing Terry was there so they could laugh at this commodification of art, as if that was all there is to it. She wonders how her fellow exhibitors feel about this and though she hasn't met them yet, too busy all hanging their work, she is sure she knows their reaction will be like her own and they'll be angry or satirical at being the gloss on an attempt to open up a new trade route to a developing country.

A dark haired girl is coming towards her with a brochure in her hands, open at the photographs and biographies of the artists. 'You are Paula Sanderson, yes?'

Paula nods.

'I have recognize you from your picture. I wish to speak with you about the picture, <u>Twinings.</u>'

Paula puts out her hand. The girl shakes it and goes on: 'I am Anesta Sandro. I too am an artist. I like very much this picture but I want to be sure one thing. These are two female forms yes? This is a gay picture?'

'Yes. If you want to see it that way.'

'You are gay or this is just being art?'

'I am. But I don't think that should make a difference to how the picture is seen. There's also an element of the double helix of DNA intertwined as, I suppose, a female principle, you could even see it as an echo of St Anne and the Virgin by Leonardo.'

'No but they make love, yes? And there are no babies, that is right. I ask for myself because it is not usual here. I am happy to meet with you. You have no drink. I get you glass of wine?'

'Thank you. That would be great. Red please.'

The girl is swallowed by the crowd of viewers. Paul wonders if she will come back or even if she wants her to. She's pretty, dark eyed and intense. Much younger than Paul. She hopes the girl isn't going to get too intrusive. She senses a neediness.

Terry would laugh. 'Why do they all, men and women, fall down for you like ninepins? Me too of course.' And then she would kiss her for reassurance.

The girl is back with two glasses of red wine. Paul says 'thank you' politely and takes a gulp at her glass. Openings are always a debilitating mix for her of excitement, fear and anti-climax. Looking round the room at the punters she thinks that she might be anywhere in Southern Europe, the same darkly glowing skin, hair and eyes.

'You are happy that I talk with you.'

'Yes of course. That's fine.'

'You see here in Mexico, even in the city, is hard to be gay for woman.'

'But I thought...Brazil..?'

'It's not like Brazil. Here is gay men okay but woman is more hide. Woman is be madre but I don't want be madre. Mia madre pray for me give her baby. What do you say..?'

'Grandchild?'

'Si. The priest tell her wait. Will be okay. But not for me. So I want come in London.'

'That's not easy now. You need a job and some capital.' Paul sees from the girl's face she hasn't understood. 'To get a visa you need employment and money in the bank.'

'I get money. I save here. You can give me work?'

'I'm afraid not. I'm just an artist. I don't have people working for me. You could apply to a language school to teach Spanish or a private school. Do you have a degree?'

'From universita, si.'

'Then that's your best bet. Write to the teaching agencies that find jobs for teachers.'

'You help me please.' The girl is looking at her intently, her dark eyes about to spill over with tears. What can she do?

'Do you have a card, your email address? I'll send you some addresses to contact.'

'Gracias, muchas gracias, muchas. See I have.' She takes a small cardboard oblong from her shoulder bag. 'I will love you always.' She lunges forward flinging her arms round Paul and kissing her twice. The bag falls to the floor spilling its innards: lipstick, compact, cigarette packet, small cylindrical lighter, cards. 'You have card for me?'

'No, but I will email you; I promise.'

'Please, you not forget.'

'I promise.'

Paul sees with relief that the British consul is being ushered towards her and, leaving the girl still scrabbling on the floor, she moves towards him.

'Ah, Miss Sanderson, you must tell me about yourself and your work. Have you been to Mexico City before?'

The next day Paul takes the bus out to Teotihuacan. 'You must go,' Terry had said. 'I've always wanted to see it.'

The bus is full and the road not made for a smooth ride. She can see why the main drag through the site is the Cazada de los Muertos; tourists could be half dead on arrival after the hour of being tossed to and fro. Paul is glad to get down and stretch her legs as she wanders among the broken palaces, with their carved and painted figures of gods and beasts, around the two great ziggorats of the sun and moon. Lawrence's plumed serpent is everywhere, along with the jaguar god in feathered headdress, the quetzal bird and the vital rain god, Tlaloc, demanding constant propitiation.

Paul is dazzled by the midday sun as she peers up from under her floppy panama, recommended by the guide book, at the stepped structures she has no wish to climb in the boiling heat, wondering at their construction while the Romans were building Verulamium. The Piramide del Sol, she reads, is built over a cavern where the later Aztecs believed the sun was worshipped, the blazing god who ripened the maize and fed his people. Olmec, Toltec, Aztec and then the so-called white man, the conquistadors, who had come to her show, and imposed their language on this bit of the continent, and now struggled to cross into the polygenic settlement the blond Saxons had made in the North, bringing their language in turn to their New World.

She lets the sights and sound sink down to the depth that her own work springs from, without consciously thinking how they might later re-emerge. Tired from the bombardment of images and the stare of the sun, Paul goes in search of food and drink, leaving the site for the Restaurant La Gruta in a dark cool cavern, before making her way back to the roundabout at Gate One and the bus for the city.

Next day after a morning spent at the gallery sitting beside her work, answering questions, Paul takes herself to the Museo Nacional de Antropologia. She wants to see as much as she can digest before flying home. Trips to Mexico don't come every year. She's glad of the shade as she strolls through the two leafy parks leading towards the museum and then past a pair of bronze lions and, in the distance, a boating lake, to the entrance.

She passes a man sweeping the paths, noticing his broad features. Then she is paying for her ticket, ignoring the offer of an audio guide, preferring just to look and read the captions in their English translations. Crossing the courtyard with its huge stone fountain dome she enters the hall where the first arrivals have made their way from the North, across the Bering Strait from Asia, and down the continent to the fertile lakeland basin of the Valle de Mexico, first hunting, then cultivating the native wild grasses, like their contemporaries on the other side of the world.

A flurry of blue and white resolves into a group of uniformed school girls, neatly in twos. Paul judges them to be about nine or ten years old, still eager children before the onset of teenage angst. They follow Paul into the preclassic hall and spread out to pass from Olmec, to Toltec, looking up at the exotic displays and suddenly, seeing their entranced faces like those of the bad guys the Indians, the hero, white of course, must defeat in Hollywood westerns, she sees that they have come to look at themselves in their past, their voices a subdued murmur, a susurration of approval sometimes rising to a higher pitched chorus like the chatter of parakeets, when they gather in front of some particularly significant display.

Then Paul moves on into the Aztec hall, the civilisation that fascinates Europe, which needs to pore over its more gruesome aspects in order to justify its own destruction of a rival. Here are more feathered gods, half human jaguars, serpents like she saw yesterday. She moves on and suddenly she's standing before two great stone heads with the distinctive features of the man she had seen sweeping the paths. 'Olmec,' the caption reads.

Lost civilisations, peoples, swirl around her. Like Terry's Picts, Paul thinks, victims of conquest or absorption as a snake ingests a frog or fledgling, survival of the fittest among humans as other animals. Traces of Neanderthal DNA in modern man. And we learn nothing, scrambling and clawing for territory, actual or virtual, land or wealth, elevating an animal necessity into a human ritual, the religion of the market place, eat or be eaten.

Suddenly Paul needs to get out, out from under history and man's inhumanity to man. Leaving the rest of the halls with their vanished societies, she steps out into the blaring sunlight and heads for an avenue of trees leading back towards the hotel. In front of her she can see a man sweeping. Is it the same? She walks slowly towards him until she can see the features of the stone statue under the shading brim of his hat.

Paul takes her phone out of her pocket and steps up to him. 'Please may I take your photograph?'

'Non hablo inglese.'

Paul holds up her phone with the lens towards him and mimes taking a picture. The man bows and smiles, sweeping off his hat with a little bow. Paul takes a couple of shots full face, profile.

'Thank you, thank you so much. Muchos gracias.'

The sweeper bows again, puts on his hat, takes up his broom and goes back to clearing the path.

⚜ ⚜ ⚜

'It's so good to have you back,' Terry said running her hand over Paul's smooth shoulder and then cupping a full breast in her palm.

'So tell me what's been going on,' Paul said punctuating her words with snatched kisses.

'Well the latest is rather as expected, the religious leaders both Catholic and evangelical Protestant have spoken out against gay marriage. They even want to put the clock right back and drop civil partnership. The government is in a mess because it miscalculated. It thought it could seize the moral high ground from the old left by playing on the Scottish Enlightenment as its historic justification.'

'I've got to move my arm,' Paul said. 'That's better. So what now?'

'They've miscalculated because the economy isn't going well. It's taking longer to get all the independent projects 'on stream' as management speak puts it. Things like wind power, reopening the Clyde shipyards, the new gas fields, and of course when things don't move fast enough you can always blame the immigrants, even though they're only providing necessary expertise, for instance the tie-in with Gdansk and investment in the Clyde, or farming those bits of land nobody else wanted for over a century. So not Caledonia the golden. But worst of all perhaps or most dangerous, is that the faith groups have now formed political parties and one threatening to stand in the next election. The Catholic Party, wants union with Ireland, the Republic; the Protestants are cosying up to the Ulster Unionists, and the PSA are using the possible splits in the mainstream parties along religious grounds to pick up support and position themselves as the real Scotland in the next election.

'Is there any more of this stuff?'

'Just that last night the old rioting between Celtic and Rangers broke out. Ever since that America Bible belt consortium rescued Rangers this has been on the cards. But it's worse than the old riots because it wasn't contained between groups of supporters. It was much bigger, with gangs being called up by mobile networks to a full scale riot, setting fire to cars and looting, that stuff! The First Minister finally called in the army.'

'I've heard enough,' Paul said. 'Let's get dressed and go and eat. Take the taste away.'

⚜ ⚜ ⚜

From <u>The Irish Times</u>

In an effort to defuse the growing sectarian violence in the cities, the First Minister of Alba will visit Daine next week, the city of Colmcille, for talks with the Taosearch and the First Minister of Ulster. It is thought they will consider the proposal for a Celtic Federation already approved by the Doyle.

Paul is heading up Queen Street towards the opulent sand-stone façade of the Gallery of Modern Art, on Royal Exchange Square, whose name embodies the gallery's former incarnation as the central money market, and before that a rich merchant's mansion. In front of the portico of Corinthian columns topped by a circular temple, clock tower, Wellington sits on his horse with a traffic cone on his head, that some thoughtful student has climbed up and put there to protect him from the attention of pigeons.

She's both excited and apprehensive. This is the first time her work has been shown in a large public gallery, in an exhibition of contemporary material by artists who aren't yet broadsheet names. Some of her students have made up a party and are meeting in the entrance, and Terry will be along later after her last seminar.

Inside the gallery is just as imposing in its industrial 19th century splendour as Manchester Town Hall, that other great relic of civic pride, operatic as a thirties picture palace in its late Georgian classicism, with more columns and sculptured plaster ceiling. Long windows and the lantern make it perfect for a gallery. Paul wonders how her work will look against this restrained yet gaudy backdrop. This time she has borrowed works from Kravic, relying on the gallery's expertise in careful shipment.

The jeaned and t-shirted band of students picks her up, and carries her along to In Our Times, set up in what was once the Newsroom, where a decent crowd is already milling past the exhibits consulting catalogues, swapping reactions or just standing silent in front of some particular piece.

'Where are yours Paula?' Alec, in a bright yellow top and red and white trainers, asks.

'Over there I think in that side gallery. But you have to look at the other work as well. We're going to talk about all of it on Friday.' But they are streaming and shoving their way forward.

They never reach it. Afterwards she can't remember if she heard the explosion. The blast hurls her to the ground amid the falling debris of painted stucco, and for a few moments she loses consciousness. When she comes to, her head is still ringing and dizzy. She tries to sit up, falls back, tries again, manages it and rests there for a minute, as she thinks, wondering if she can stand. She knows she's bruised and her nostrils and mouth are full of the stink of explosive and old dust. At first she seems at to be deaf. Then gradually sounds begin to come to her, at first sounding as if from a distance, then louder, close by, moaning and crying. She must try to stand up. She turns over on all fours and raises herself up with her hands against the floor, gets one foot down and pushes up slowly, her legs threatening to buckle and drop her back again. Then she is standing, looking down at her torn jeans, but reassuringly there's no sign of blood. She dares to look around.

There are bodies strewn about the room, with here and there a dazed sitting or standing figure. Some she can only make out as an arm or leg sticking out from a heap of rubble, smashed wood and glass. One shape lies under a heavy wooden bench upended over it like a beached boat or crushing carapace.

She moves towards where she had last seen the students and begins pulling at a mound of rubble partly covering a yellow t-shirt. Sickened she sees a red and white trainer lying nearby. She begins to try to lift off the lumps of rubble, uncovering his head first. His eyes are closed but he's still breathing. Does the world outside know what's happening or are they on their own in the shattered room? She tears more pieces of carved pediment from the tops of broken columns from the boy's body, squeezing dust and plaster out of his nose and mouth to let him breathe more easily. 'Come on Alec, wake up! Open your eyes.' She hears an alarm begin to sound. Surely someone will come now.

'You alright Paula?' One of the students is bending over her. Laura she thinks is the girl's name.

'I'm ok. You? Help me get this stuff off Alec. You start with his legs. I'll carry on up here.'

Laura bends over the boy, tossing aside small lumps of plaster. 'Can you help me with this big bit?'

A whole coved section of moulding is obscuring his legs under the small stuff. They take an end each and lift carefully. Laura lets out a little cry as they expose the shattered bloody mess of first one leg, and then the other, twisted under him. Paul puts her arms round his shoulders and cradles him against her. 'Come on, open your eyes,' She says again. The eyelids flutter for a moment then droop again.

Suddenly there's a different noise. Strong voices shouting orders, the crunch of boots on plaster. 'Okay then. Let's have the laddie.' And Alec is lifted onto a stretcher. 'You'd best get yourselves out of here if you's can walk.'

Everywhere bodies are being lifted or supported towards the door. Paul hears the ringing bells of fire engines. Is the gallery on fire? 'Come on,' she says to Laura, 'we'd better get out.'

'Will he be alright, Alec?'

'He's young, and fit I think. He should be okay in time.'

'I feel a bit sick.'

'Here, give me your arm. We'll help each other.'

⚜   ⚜   ⚜

Terry had just turned into Queen Street as the fire engines roared past on a wave of sirens. People began running along the pavements after them or stood staring up the road towards Royal Exchange Square. Terry too begins to run, with a sickening premonition of some disaster. She turns the corner only to come up against a wall of backs, a crowd of people staring towards the right hand side of the square.

'What is it? What's happened.'

'Someone said there's been an explosion in the gallery. A bomb they think.'

❧ ❧ ❧

Next morning Paul couldn't get out of bed. Terry had finally managed to push her way to the front of the crowd only to be stopped by a police cordon.

'You canna gae in there Miss.'

'I must. My partner's in there.'

'He'll be out soon enough. Just you wait quiet. See, they're bringing them out now.'

A convoy of stretchers and walking wounded was appearing under the portico where an ambulance stood with rear doors open. Then she saw Paul limping out giving an arm to a girl who kept stumbling and nearly falling. Terry saw an ambulance attendant step forward and put his arm round the girl while exchanging a few words with Paul. Then he led the girl gently away and Paul resumed her slow limp down the shallow steps to the pavement.

'Paul, over here! I'm here!'

Terry had insisted on a taxi though Paul had said she was okay, nothing broken.

'You ought to get checked out at a-and-e.'

'I'm fine. Just a few bruises I expect. I just want to get home.'

It as true she was bruised but miraculously not broken. The explosion, for that was what it was now being called, had killed one guide who had died from a heart attack, and injured many others, some of whom were said to be either 'stable' or sinisterly 'critical' in hospital. Paul wondered as they watched the local news how the boy, Alec, was being described. She hoped for the comforting 'stable'. Then the newscaster was saying: 'We understand that the explosion is being claimed by a group previously unknown to the police and the security forces as a protest against 'decadent foreign art'. We will bring you more on this development as we get it. The Security forces' spokesperson has described it as a worrying development. Is this the rise of cultural terrorism? If so it will be difficult to combat without increasing the security checks on visitors too, at, for instance, galleries and museums, perhaps even theatres and cinemas to an unacceptable level akin to those at airports. People will simply stop going, and perhaps that is the intention to impoverish the cultural life of the nation.'

Paul lay in bed not sure whether she was unable or just unwilling to get up.

'I said you should have gone to the hospital.' Terry picked up the cup of tea she had brought, now grown cold, undrunk on the table at Paul's side of the bed.

'I'm sorry. I want to go home.'

'You mean back to London?'

'Hm.'

'Wait a few days until you're a bit stronger then I'll come with you.'

'No you stay here. You've got your classes. I'll be fine on my own. Promise.' Paul said, looking at Terry's worried face. She felt detached from this body that wouldn't obey her will and lift her off the bed. Yet at the same time she could imagine herself on a train going away from yesterday's horror, opening the door of the flat, and shutting it behind her on the world with herself safely inside.

'You will come back won't you?'

'Of course. I just need time for it to, not go away, it may not ever do that. Subside that's the only word I can think of now.'

'Okay, you rest. Try to sleep. I'll bring you some soup later. When you're ready in a day or two I'll drive you into Glasgow for a train.'

'Thanks darling. I'm sorry I'm being so wet.'

'You're not 'wet'. You're in shock still. Traumatised like a soldier would be. Now sleep.'

Paul dozed on and off through the day, images from the blasted gallery forcing themselves into her dreams and her waking; things she didn't even consciously remember seeing. Were they actual memories, or fictions constructed from news clips, photos and descriptions of other maimed or dead? She tried not to think about what had happened but they rose up like phantoms were supposed to do, terrorising the living.

'Would you rather have the bed to yourself tonight?' Terry asked. 'I could get out the sofa bed.'

'Would you mind? I think I'm better on my own at the moment.' She felt as if something had broken inside, leaving her numb, disconnected. Terry's concern and her own inability to respond to it only made the sensation worse. Logically she knew Terry was right: she was in shock, turned almost to stone by the experience. Some lines kept going through her head:

'Most like a monumental statue set...

Touch it; the marble eyelids are not wet:

If it could weep it could arise and go.'

'It,' that was it: she felt an it, stripped of her humanity, refusing to admit that she had anything in common with those who had done this, could do this.

She hoped that next morning she would be able to get up, to move her limbs, attempt solid food but the feeling of distance, of alienation didn't go away. 'I think I'll be well enough to go tomorrow if you can drive me to the station.'

'Okay Baby. If that's best for you.'

Terry closed the door and went downstairs to pour herself a glass of wine before unfolding the sofa-bed. She was still trying to adjust, to take in the depths of Paul's trauma. Was she treating it right? Telling Paul to pull herself together, that after all she wasn't injured, apart from bruising and stiffness, only deeply internally, psychologically wounded, didn't seem like an option.

But the feeling of an ending, of separation wouldn't go away, the doubt that attends on love, in the words of an old popsong that floated through her consciousness: 'Will you still love me tomorrow?' or Shakespeare's universal: 'Since why to love poor me I can allege no cause'. She wanted to howl but knew she mustn't. That could come later when she was alone, when Paul was gone.

She promised herself she wouldn't beg, wouldn't say again: 'You will come back won't you?' dreading a cold or equivocal reply, an: 'Of course,' spoken without feeling or worse a 'maybe', dressed up in its own cloak of words, veiling the true meaning.

Next morning she looked up the timetable, got out a small bag that Paul could carry and drove her to the station. 'Don't come onto the platform. I hate goodbyes,' Paul said.

'You're sure you can manage?'

'I'm much better.'

'Let me know you got home safely.'

'Of course.'

They hugged. Paul walked away through the barrier. On the other side she turned back to wave, then began to diminish down the length of the platform while Terry stood, watching her recede until she turned towards the steps up to an open carriage door and vanished inside. Then Terry too turned towards the exit, the held back tears choking in her throat and nostrils. Inside the car she leant her head on the steering wheel, and now she howled, not able to drive away while her eyes were blurred and her nose running. It was some time before she felt confident enough to turn the key and start the engine for the lonely drive back to the empty cottage.

❧ ❧ ❧

Paul opened the door and stepped inside the flat. It smelt faintly musty and unlived in, unloved. Crossing Blackfriars Bridge she had felt the lift in spirits the return to London, epitomised by her first sight of the Thames and the skyline on both sides, up and down river, always gave her, but it had faded as the bus trundled through South London. Now her feeling of loss returned. She bent to pick up the detritus of junk mail and went through into the sitting room where a dead Busy Lizzie rebuked her from the windowsill.

She dug her notebook out of a drawer and powered it up. She hadn't felt well enough to face her inbox since the bombing, dreading to find out what had happened to the students in her care, as if she was somehow responsible for the whole event. Now she saw an email from Loren, a girl who hadn't been there but was part of the group. Flicking down it she saw the name she had been dreading: Alec. She didn't want to see the news that he was dead or maimed for life.

'Hi Paula,

Hope you're ok. Heard you got caught in the blast at the gallery. Hope it's nothing serious. Someone said they thought you'd gone back to London. I do hope you'll come back. You were great for us and I love your work. We all appreciate the input you give our seminars.

Some of the gang who were there are still off, gone home to recover or just using it as an excuse to skive off but only Alec of our lot was actually injured like some other people were, and the woman who was killed of course. I think she was an attendant. Anyway Alec, they say, will be ok and they can fix his legs so he can walk though he has to have mega-surgery.

Hope to see you soon. Loren.'

Underneath was another email from Flora at her gallery, filled with alarm and concern, and one from Kiril Kravic hoping she wasn't injured and that his current show was pulling in the crowds. Paul knew she must answer them all but not yet. She picked up the corpse of the dead plant and took it through to the kitchen where she emptied its coffin pot of dried out compost and shrivelled leaves into the bin. Then she wandered from room to room, opening windows and the door to the tangled jungle that the garden had become, neglected under the summer rain. Tomorrow she would get a fresh plant.

Inside her conservatory studio door, she stared around at the silence without recognition. What did she do here?

She felt rather than heard her mobile phone buzzing in her pocket.

'Sorry, I just wondered if you were home yet,' Terry's voice sounded unsure, hesitant.

'Just got in. That boy, Alec, he's going to be okay. It's such a relief.'

'Will you…will you be okay?'

Paul felt a sudden lift, as if a chain had been severed, allowing her to move and breathe and feel.

'I'll be okay. I'm feeling better. Don't worry about me, about us. I love you.' Suddenly she felt the relief of tears. 'It's alright.'

' What will you do this evening?'

'First I'm going to make a cup of tea, if we've got some long life milk. What could be more prosaic than that?'

But when the call ended Paul stood motionless for a moment. Then she took an already primed board from the stack by the wall and put it on the easel. This wasn't a time for ephemera; she wanted the permanence and authority of paint. It was a time for Guernica, Kronos devouring his children, The Sleep of Reason. For Picasso, Goya, Blake. She began to sketch blackly on the white ground.

⚜ ⚜ ⚜

'I shouldn't have asked her to come up here,' Terry thought, 'but I couldn't know then what would happen, how it would all work out. It seemed so simple. And now...' She was watching the television news unfold.

'The bombing of the Modern Art Gallery has been claimed by a group calling themselves the Alban Cultural and Heritage League, or AHCL, to preserve 'the purity of Alban culture.'

The next day the few remaining papers were full of it but it was hard to tell if they were for or against. To them it was just a way to sell more papers, menaced by the on-line Newsday threat. So few of them were left now, and the rest were simply hanging on, their influence on public opinion far beyond their sales figures, aided and abetted by their morning radio airing as people hurried to leave for work.

'I've started a new picture,' Paul said when Terry rang her before setting off for work.

'Good for you.' But she felt a rush of anxiety again. Last night she had been reassured but now if Paul had begun work at the flat it meant she wasn't coming back soon. She would want to make up for what she had lost.

'It's very big and complex.'

Terry's heart sank further. 'I'll have to go or I'll miss the ferry. I'm going to call in on the office tonight to see what they make of it all. I'll ring when I'm back. Good luck with the picture.'

She found her first class strangely hushed. There was a feeling of tension, of shared apprehension. This morning was the Culture and Politics seminar which Terry usually began tactfully by suggesting that to label the brilliant group of 15th and 16th century Scottish writers, Scottish Chaucerians, was itself a political act, that Dunbar and Henryson in particular were their own makers. But when she came to quote from James I of Scotland's own Spring Song:

Worship ye that lovers been this May

she found her voice about to break. Abruptly she cut the verse short and asked for comments, questions.

'Do you think they'll try to do here what they did at the gallery?' one student asked, and Terry suddenly understood that the tension she had felt was fear.

'Why do that?' someone else said, 'why take it out on inanimate objects, works of art? That's just vandalism.'

'Doesn't it say something about the intrinsic nature of art, that it has meaning, that it carries, for example, people's identity, their aspirations! It's not just a pretty bauble or even a marketable commodity. When a faith or a political system, or country takes over another it tries to destroy that meaning. Think of Hitler burning books and works of art, banning Jewish composers, Protestants destroying icons, Roundheads hacking away at statues, Muslim extremists demolishing statues of the Buddha...I don't think the university is at risk. Don't we have a recognised branch of the PSA among our political societies?'

'Aye but when has that ever stopped anyone? That would just make them martyrs.'

'I'm sure the Principal and the authorities are aware of any possibility of that kind, and are stepping up security. Obviously we all have to be careful and thankful that term only has a few more weeks to run.'

But that evening at the party office she put the same question: Was this a one off or the beginning of a campaign?

'Who are these ACHL?' She asked Jim McClellan.

'They call themselves the cultural wing of the PSA.'

'That figures then. So they're the equivalent of the English warm beer and old maids cycling to church brigade, but with bombs?'

'More like the EDL who go in for bombing mosques and gay pubs.'

'What about the Scottish Colourists?' Terry said, remembering something Paul had told her. 'Are they okay?'

'No. They're decadent, foreign influenced.'

'Who's left then? Elizabeth Blackadder?' Paul was an unashamed admirer of her work, Terry knew.

'Hell no. Too feminine. Cats and flowers. They want something more macho.'

'The artistic equivalent of tossing the caber. That's surely the most phallic sport of all.'

Jim McClellan laughed. 'I don't think I'll quote you on that Terry.'

❧ ❧ ❧

AD 600

Although no women were allowed on Hy for fear the novices might be distracted from the love of God, yet Colm had compassion on the suffering of women. For, as he once said to me, the Lord was born of a woman or he would not have been very man, and also although women are less than men in that Eve who betrayed us all was only formed of one rib of Adam, yet the mother of Christ redeemed that betrayal in giving her first born to die for us.

So knowing that his kinswoman was nearing her time to be delivered of her first born, and that she would be in great pain and in fear for her life and that of the child, and that she would call upon him for aid since she was of his mother Eithne's family, Colm arose from his reading and ran to the church to pray for her.

Then when he came out of the church he told those of us who had gone to meet him, that she was safely delivered in Scotia, through the compassion and help of Our Lord born of a woman. And this was later confirmed by travellers bringing news from her part of Scotia.

Yet again he sent help to another woman in Scotia Hibernica who called upon him in her pain. At first light one morning on Hy he summoned me and told me to make the curragh ready for a journey I was to make to Scotia.

'The holy virgin Magain, daughter of Daimene, coming home from church after the night office fell, and has broken her hip in two places. Take this little pinewood box. Inside is my blessing. When you visit Magain dip the blessing in a flask of water, pour this water over her hip and it will be healed. Look, on this box I will write the number of years, twenty three, which she will live after she is cured.'

So I set sail and arrived at Diamene, her father's house. As instructed I took the blessing out of the box and steeped it in water. Then I was shown into the room where the holy virgin lay in great pain. I told her that Colm had sent me with a cure for her hip. So turning back the bed covering and laying her on her good side, she pointed to her hip under its white gown and I proceeded to pour the water over it, both of us calling upon the name of the Lord. And instantly she felt the bone knit together, and was filled with joy and gratitude that I had come as Colm's messenger. And as I afterwards heard she lived another twenty-three years in great holiness among the people.

On another occasion as I heard from one of the brothers, Genereus, a Saxon and the baker for the community, that Colm had praised a happy woman, a wife whose soul the angels had carried up to heaven where she fought with the demons who had taken the soul of her husband, a layman and not a believer but righteous, and triumphed over them by her love and virtue so that they two were reunited for eternity.

Yet he could be stern with a woman who had refused to sleep with her husband on Rathlin Island and had offered instead to cross the sea and enter a monastery for women.

But Colm said it was unlawful to put apart those whom God had joined and made one flesh. 'Today we will fast and pray, the three of us together.' That night while they slept after their day of fasting and prayer, Colm continued to pray for them, and in the morning when he asked if she still wished to go away to a woman's monastery she answered that her heart had melted from hate to love and now she wished to stay with her husband, and so she remained ever after.

⚜ ⚜ ⚜

201?

From the International Financial News July 14th

The city is buzzing with rumours that both of Britain's biggest banks are to move their headquarters abroad to

Hong Kong and Mumbai. The two have not been positively identified but William Hill is already taking bets on possible candidates. It is thought that the Treasury has imposed a blackout on the names for fear it might cause panic and a run on the whole financial sector. With the increased confidence in the Eurozone, sparked by the revival of the Mediterranean countries' economies through the greater federation of fiscal policies which has enabled them to invest in tourism and the production of luxury goods for Asian markets, Italian fashion, French food and wine, other British financial institutions are said to be looking to Frankfurt and even Helsinki for possible relocation.

Meanwhile the Scottish government has made an offer to take RBS, with its subsidiaries NatWest and the Ulster Bank, off the major shareholder, British government's, hands for an undisclosed sum, following the discovery of a large gas field off the Western Isles, and the link up as a Celtic Fuels Federation with the new oil fields off the Irish coast, which rely heavily on Scottish know-how and long experience in North Sea exploration, with new rigs being built at Govan. This has enabled Scotland to borrow the necessary billions of Euros from the ECB to effect the purchase. Given the state of the British economy it is thought the government will jump at the chance to offload its share in RBS, in return for hard cash. Who knows: this may set a precedent. Maybe the Welsh will make a bid for Lloyds, now that carbon capture is an economic reality, allowing for the resumed exploration of deep and opencast mining, and fracking.

⚜ ⚜ ⚜

AD 600

On Hy there was neither Scot nor Pict, nor Briton nor Saxon, only those who had chosen the Lord's way, and on that way all were equal. So it was that the Saxon Pilu was witness to a moment in Colm's life when only two were present, and when Colm believed he was to be translated out of this life. With the Saxon Pilu was also Lugneus Mocoblai, an Hibernian Scot, and both were standing at the door of Colm's hut when they saw within his face, first light up with joy and then transfixed with an overwhelming sadness.

Seeing his distress they begged to know what had caused him first such joy, then to be so suddenly changed. 'Do not ask,' Colm said, 'but go on your way in peace.' But they fell upon their knees weeping and asking again to be told what had happened.

Then Colm seeing their great grief swore them to silence. 'Because I love you I do not want to distress you. You must first promise never to tell anyone of the blessing I have received while I am still alive.' They at once agreed to do as he had asked and, when they had agreed, Colm continued. 'This day marks the 30th year since I began my pilgrimage in Britain. Many years ago I asked God that at the end of 30 years he would release me from my earthly home and call me to the heavenly kingdom. And this was the reason for my joy about which you asked me, for I saw angels descending from the holy seat to free my soul from the flesh. But now see they are suddenly stopped and stand on the rocks on the other side of the strait from our island, as if wanting to call from my body. But they are not allowed to come any closer and must turn their steps back towards heaven. Although the Lord had given me what I had prayed for with all my might, that this day I should go from this world to him, he has heard the prayers of many churches about me, and has at once changed his mind. For these churches have offered prayers to the Lord that, even though it is against my desire, that from today I should remain in the flesh for another four years. This delay, so sad delay, is the cause of my understandable grief today. However, when these four years have passed, by God's kindness, I shall die quickly without any preceding physical suffering, with the holy angels coming to meet me at the appointed time, and I shall go gladly to the Lord.'

All this was told me by the Saxon Pilu after Colm's death, for he had kept his vow till then, and before he went back to his own people to help in their enlightening in the way of the Lord, for as he told me, most among them were still pagan although there were Christians among their Pict neighbours since the time of the holy Ninian's labours on the North East coast. And now he heard that monks had been sent from Rome and were preaching to the Saxon people in the South of the country, and he was anxious to join them in their task.

⚜ ⚜ ⚜

201?

Paul and Terry are on the video link. 'When are you coming down?' Paul asks.

Terry hesitates. Sometimes the old mobiles were better when you couldn't see each other's faces. 'I feel I've got to stay here at the moment and see this through.'

Paul is trying to seem calm and not to let her rising panic show. She's in danger of breaking, and hopes Terry's reception isn't so good that she can spot the signs. 'Why, what's happening?'

'An unholy coalition of religious freaks or, I suppose I should be tolerant and say extremists, and xenophobes. Anti almost everything you and I would think reasonable. They forced a vote of confidence in the government yesterday which the government lost and now has to call an election. Meanwhile they've already ramped up their campaign, against immigrants and gays, and to bring back national service. They want to abolish the gay marriage law the government passed with what was a sizable majority and then get rid of civil partnerships. And they've linked up with other right wing and similar groups in Europe since they got a couple of Europeans seats in the parliament. They're also misogynist: they want to make it illegal for women to use contraception or have an abortion without the husband or father's written consent.'

'I can't imagine many Scotswomen putting up with that. But I think that's maybe all too much for you to take on. You ought to come home.'

'Oh I'm not alone and I'd feel such a wet if I just turned and ran.'

'Who said: 'He who fights and runs away...?'

'Could you come up for a bit?'

'I don't think I'm quite ready for that yet.'

'It's going on a long time darling. Are you sure you don't need some help?'

'Oh you know my worry about that. Mess with the mind and maybe the work goes away. Who'd be a bloody artist?'

'I love you.'

'I love you too. It'll be alright. Just give me a bit more time. Maybe we could have a weekend.'

'Oh fuck the politics for a couple of days. I'll come down on Friday and go back Sunday night. Classes start on Monday and I'm on at nine o'clock. I'm sorry we never made it to Greece.'

'That was my fault. I just wasn't ready for it.' She hadn't felt brave enough, had wanted just to shut herself away, to work on IED which now covers a whole wall of her studio. What had begun as a painting is now a vast collage against the painted ground embodying Adomnan's text of 697, the Law of the Innocents, laying down the giving of compensation for civilian casualties like Alec whose bloodied body is at the centre of the work in effigy. 'Kravic is coming over sometime this week to look at my new picture since it's too big to move, and anyway I don't know if it's finished yet.'

'I hope you've got your anti-grope spray ready.'

'Will you really come down at the weekend?'

'You just be ready.'

Paul is smiling as she switches off her mobile. Back in the cottage Terry feels a flood of desire, thinking of how they will make love, roused by her own evocation, wondering, hoping it has had the same effect on Paul.

Kravic announces his intention of taking Paul to lunch when he arrives next morning. To get the viewing off on the right foot Paul agrees, offers him coffee or a glass of wine, both of which he refuses in his impatience to see the new work and, having got that over, make her some kind of proposition over lunch which she senses is his main reason for coming.

She leads him towards her studio, being careful to keep a physical space between them, opens the door and stands back so that the work dominating the wall opposite can make its full impact.

Kravic stands for a couple of moments staring at it. 'This not what you make usual.'

'No, maybe not.'

'Always I like in your work the English humour. This very black.'

'It was a very black experience.'

'Ah yes. You tell me: the bomb. Let us go and eat and. I talk to you more. I have book table at Browns. We go tube to Leicester Square. Come.'

At least, Paul thinks, there's safety in a public space as long as he doesn't play footsie under the table.

'I'm sorry you don't like my new work,' Paul says as they walk to the Oval Station, past the Green, and the great Victorian Church islanded from the traffic in its own oasis of trees, towards the egg shaped cricket ground carved out of a mesh of streets.

Paul is relieved to see that the restaurant is too crowded for real intimacy. Kravic had tried to take her arm in the short distance from Leicester Square tube to St Martin's lane but she had managed to push ahead fearing that the hand on her arm would also take the opportunity to be crushed against her breast.

'Now we are having the wine,' he said when they had been directed to a table. And when it came he went on raising his glass to chink against hers: 'Now I tell you secret.'

'About the new picture…'

'I don't speak of picture. I speak of new gallery. Picture is too big for here. You too big for here. You come in Geneva.'

'Why would I do that? How do you mean?'

'I open up big new gallery in Geneva where is now the money. Not here any more. London finish. Everyone leave. You come live in Geneva. I buy big black picture for half a million, sell for one million.'

'There's no resale right in Switzerland.'

'You don't need. You make, I make you, plenty money without resale right. Just four percent! Peanuts!'

Paul thinks she should just get up and leave now. But suddenly she is boneachingly weary, weary of the whole struggle. 'I'm afraid that's not on, Kiril. You see I couldn't work there.'

'Why not? You work in Scotland before the bomb.'

'That's different. Whatever the politics it's not foreign, not abroad. It's still part of me.'

'You don't like to cross the water. You island people.'

'I don't mind if I know I'm coming back. After all I went to Mexico and found that very stimulating. Very different you see, but also a very old culture and yet still very vibrant.'

'And you think Geneva not vibrant?'

'I don't know. I've never been there. But I know I'm not comfortable with an aggressively money- based ethos.'

'You artists can be the idealist while we have to make money to support you.'

'But without us, our silly idealism, you don't make the money. You need us to give you something to sell. But it's still ours. In a way, though the physical object goes, it's still ours in essence. Rather, I imagine, like when a child leaves home.'

'Ah, the female view of art.'

'No, I know male artists, authors of all sorts, who feel just the same. It's easier for musicians, composers, because even if they send their work out to be played, everyone can see that it's still theirs. It's more tenuous with us because it may be the unique object that we give up. But we feel the same.'

'So I am not persuading you to come to Switzerland then. But I shall take your work and you will never see it again. And the new black picture. I will still buy from you so that no one else can take it. And I will hang it in my new gallery for all the world to come to. And they will respect it because it is so strong.' He signalled to the waiter for the bill.

Paul feels a pang of loss. She wants to say: 'No, you can't have it! But she knows that would be a stupid gesture. She needs the money now she no longer has the visiting lecture-ship blown away by the bomb blast. When she feels stronger she will begin scouring the papers for something else, look-ing up old contacts, applying for the meagre grants avail-able. But for now she says: 'I'll let you know when it's fin-ished. I have a bit more work to do on it still.'

❧ ❧ ❧

This is the News From the West Country on BBC West

Newscaster: 'Reports are coming in that activists have seized Tintagel Castle on the west coast of Cornwall, the iconic site of King Arthur's round table. They claim to be members of the KIP, Kernow Independence Party, formed by the amalgamation of various dissident Cornish groups, Kernow being the Gaelic form of Cornwall. The last Cornish Gaelic speaker is thought to have died at the end of the eighteenth century. The activists have raised the black and white flag of St Piran, who gives his name to the coastal village of Perranporth, above the castle walls. They also claim to have mined the steep stairway which provides the only access on foot to the top of the mount and the castle remains. Our reporter Neil Tregannon is on the beach below. Neil what can you see?'

Tregannon: 'There's a police helicopter hovering overhead, and that would be the only way in if there was an attempt to take the protesters out. Unless an army assault team trained in rock climbing could make an attempt to scale the cliff but that would be highly dangerous. The group here said they are armed and would resist any moves to bring them down by force. '

Newscaster: 'How are they communicating with the outside world and what do they want?'

Tregannon: 'They're using the social media as usual on these occasions. Their spokesperson, Helen Boscastle, if that is her real name, has said that they want to draw attention to the economic collapse in the South West, the neglect by London, and they're demanding assemblies for Cornwall and Devon, Kernow and Dewnans, in their terms, so that they can manage their own affairs. In particular now that Great Britain is no longer bound by European fishing quotas, they see potential in developing an independent fishing industry, expanding round the world from Plymouth by air, specializing in locally caught and prepared Kernow delicacies. They also want to take over the marketing abroad of tourism and develop the infrastructure to support it, including local airports. They say all this would provide jobs in an area of chronic unemployment, one of the two most deprived in Britain, so that they can keep their young people in the Duchy.'

Newscaster: 'But where is the money to come from for all this, do they say?'

Tregannon: 'They're appealing to private sponsors who have some connection to the area to set up an investment fund, principally American, Canadian or Australians who have Cornish ancestry. They say that it's London politicians' fault for taking us out of the EU regional development funding.'

Newscaster: 'And how are the authorities expected to respond? After all they can't allow an illegal occupation to go on.'

Tregannon: 'It's thought that the first step will be for English Heritage who own the site, to apply for a court order for their eviction.'

Newscaster: 'Do you, does anyone, think they'll take any notice of that?'

Tregannon: 'No. But it would give any assault by police or the army a legal basis.'

Newscaster: 'Do we know what sort of arms, weapons, they've got there?'

Tregannon: 'Not really. But unfortunately you can bring down a helicopter, which seems to be the only way in, with just small arms fire if it's accurate enough. Hang on a minute I've got something coming through on the other line. The authorities are bringing in a negotiator. They don't know who yet, or at least they won't say, but they claim it's to avoid bloodshed or damage to the historic monument.'

Newscaster: 'Thanks Neil. We'll come back to you later in the programme if there are any further developments. Just before you go who was St Piran? I'm sure, like me, most viewers will never have heard of him.'

Tregannon: 'Yes, well, even I had to look him up, and my family comes from Cornwall. You know the old rhyme;

By Tre, Pol and Pen

You may know they are Cornishmen.

Apparently, the story goes, he was a Cornish monk in the fifth century who went to Ireland where he was thrown off a cliff by local pagans, floated across to Cornwall on a millstone that they had tied to him, and founded his own monastery, discovered Cornish tin by heating the rocks, which turned black, and let out a trickle of molten tin. Except of course that the Greeks and the Romans before him knew all about Cornish tin and called these, at least the Greeks did, 'the Tin Islands'.'

Newscaster: 'Which accounts for the flag?'

Tregannon: 'Black for soot and burnt rock, and white for the tin.'

⚜ ⚜ ⚜

'It isn't looking too good,' Terry said. 'The polls suggest there's been a swing to the right wing coalition playing the nationalist and religious cards.'

'Like America in fact. I thought the Scots had more sense.'

'A lot of them do still of course but there's been an influx of campaigners mostly from the States and they've also managed to get hold of a couple of TV channels when their franchises came up and use them to put their message across, as well as the social networks of course. You know: Telly evangelism. That sort of thing; mixing politics with religion.'

'You will be careful won't you.'

'Oh I don't think there's any physical danger. I think your bomb was a one-off by a splinter group. At least now they've all joined forces and think they've got a political future, they don't need to make that kind of statement.'

'I hope you're right. Last weekend was lovely. '

'For me too.'

They had lain in bed after making love, listening to a bird chirring outside and the courting burble of a wood pigeon, as they watched small clouds passing across an unusually blue sky, and felt the soft touch of smooth flesh on flesh.

When she had switched off the phone at the end of the call, Terry wandered from room to room, remembering. It had been hard to get back on the train to come North, with each station it drew into and then left, another milestone away and towards the emptiness of the cottage.

'What will you do now Kravic is shutting up shop and moving to Switzerland?' she had asked Paul.

'Well I've still got my old gallery and Flora. She's been very good and understanding, stuck by me in spite of Kravic's muscling in. I think she suspected he wouldn't last but would follow the money. Then I'll have to look for some teaching, part time. Maybe the City Lit would have me back.'

'That was years ago. Hard work and badly paid. What about the Open University?'

'Is that any better? I'm keeping my eye open for artist-in-residence adverts.'

Terry was aware at once of a feeling of tension when she walked into the lecture room next morning. As she crossed the front of the room towards the desk her eye was caught by a flash of white. Someone had draped a flipchart, the sort she sometimes used to put up a doughnut or piechart or a series of events, across the metal stand. On the otherwise bare sheet was scrawled in very black letters, the thickness a felt pen would make: No Foreign Dykes Here.

Going up to the stand Terry saw that the felt pen had been left on the ledge below. Picking it up she threw back the top sheet and wrote: 'Why Not?' The room burst into spontaneous clapping and shouts of approval. Then she threw back her own inscribed sheet and wrote on the one underneath the day's topic: The Politics of Reformation.

She and Paul had watched the storming of Tintagel on the news as troops were dropped in by parachute, and a bomb disposal team located and defused the improvised mine. There had been the inevitable bloodshed, casualties stretchered away, winched up to the waiting helicopters. A last ditch attempt at blowing up the castle remains had been foiled, the white cross on a black background hauled down to cheers from the victors, while the remaining unwounded, still-standing protesters were handcuffed down the long steep staircase to the beach and a waiting police launch.

'What next?' Paul had said.

⚜ ⚜ ⚜

At the annual summer party for local activists, Terry found herself for the first time just another member, no longer the representative. The post independence election had ended with one of the majority party representing the area for the first time on a nation-wide tide of patriotic euphoria.

'We're hoping you'll stand for the local council,' the chair had said.

'Do you think we've got a chance?'

'Here in the town yes. If you mean for the parliament I doubt it. The nationalists are too new here. People will wait to give them a chance to show what they can do.'

'But what about the PSA and the new coalition?'

'I hope to God not. Not here anyway. This has always been small 'c' conservative, not given to histrionics. At least not in politics. We go a bit daft on the kilts and pipes for the Highland Gathering but that's spectacle, like Morris dancing. It's not an attempt to turn back the clock. And as for the religious bit well we've every kind of kirk here and they've always got on, but they're not minded to take over the town and discourage the day trippers.'

Terry hasn't told Paul about the episode with the flip chart. She wonders whether any word of it has reached Jane Sims or the Principal, and whether she should tell them or keep quiet, in the belief that it was an isolated incident or even a bit of a joke as evidenced by the class's response to her own action. Even so she felt an uneasiness in the corridors and classes. Was she being very oversensitive or were there whispers, looks, broken-off conversations when she walked into the room? Did other members of staff feel the same?

'I've agreed to stand for the Council,' she told Paul. 'Is that okay?'

'If that's what you feel you should do, you must.' It would mean their seeing less of each other. Could they survive or would they just drift apart? 'Think of how it used to be before we got hooked on instant communication: sailors away for year-long voyages, coming back with a half token, hoping the other half could still match it while the woman waited with her pocketed half, not knowing, fearing like in the song:

'But the other half lies now beneath the sea..."

'I'll still be able to come down of course, even if I'm elected and that isn't at all in the bag.'

'I've sold IED to Kravic. Not for half a million though. That had other strings attached.'

'Oh baby, did you have to? Couldn't you have kept it?'

'He offered me the best price ever. I thought we might need it now I'm not teaching and everything seems so uncertain. Who knows? If he makes a big splash with it, it might lead to a commission. He'll want to get rid of it. He thinks it's very dark.'

'When does it have to go?'

'I've got a couple more weeks work on it as I told him.'

'I must come down and see it; take some pictures. Why is he so keen to go?'

'He says London's finished as an art market now the big finance people are pulling out. 'The rats are deserting the sinking ship,' I told him, but he didn't get it.'

'Just as well or he might not have wanted to pay so much.'

✤ ✤ ✤

AD 600

Once when Colm was in his hut writing, there came to him Luigbe moccu Min, a Hibernian, as messenger from the King of the Strathclyde Britons, Rhyddarch of Tadwal who had many enemies. This king was famed even in Hibernia for his great devotion to the faith and for his great open-handedness, for which he was called 'Largus', and the study of the faith was upheld throughout his land so that he was known in British as rwyfadar ffyd. And for this reason he was Colm's friend and had sent his messenger to him in his need.

His enemies among the Britons were Gwenddolu and Merdin, and among the Scotti of Dal Riata, King Aedan. Now Colm was staying on the island of Hinba some ten years after the death of Diarmit, last of the pagan Kings of Hibernia when in a vision, repeated over three nights, he was commanded to ordain this Aedan, king on Hy. Colm had always favoured his brother Eoganan. The visiting angel had in his hand a book of glass which Colm took and began to read. In it he was commanded to ordain Aedan which

Colm refused to do. Then the visiting angel struck Colm with a whip across the face so that he bore the scar ever after, threatening to strike him again if he remained stubborn. So on the third night of visitation Colm accepted God's will and returned to Hy where he found Aedan already waiting. Before he laid hands on Aedan to ordain him, Colm prophesied that he and his descendants would prosper as long as neither the king nor his successors should commit any act of treachery against Colm or his Kin in Ireland: 'For if they should follow evil advice the wrath of God's angel which he has inflicted on me, shall be turned against them and they will lose the Kingship.'

But to the British King Rhyddarch he sent this very different message. First he questioned the messenger Luigbe about the King, his people and his Kingdom. But Luigbe growing impatient said in great sadness: 'Why are you asking so much about this unhappy man who does not know the hour when he will be killed by his enemies nor can he know what way he will die?'

Then at once, taking pity on him, Colm replied: 'He will never be betrayed into the hands of his enemies but will die in his own home peacefully on his pillow.' The fortress of King Rhyddarch is in Dumbarton, called the Rock of the Clyde in their tongue, and some say near where St Patrick was born and taken captive to Hibernia, and it is often threatened by the Saxons of the East who would have taken it from the Britons but they are not helped by the Lord because they are pagans still.

❧ ❧ ❧

201?

Yesterday in the Welsh Assembly.

Following its recent election success which gave the party its first ever majority in the Senedd it was no surprise when Plaid Cymri succeeded in voting for tax and spending rights for the Assembly. What is not clear is whether the Assembly has the power to assume these functions which would make them independent of the Westminster Treasury, and by extension the Bank of England and the FSA, or whether they have to be granted by Westminster as was done in the case of Scotland, in an attempt to ward off secession from the Union. In that case, as we know, it failed. People will want to know, or at least will speculate, whether a similar grant in Wales would merely prelude the same result.

It is significant that although previous opinion polls have shown little appetite among the Welsh for independence, the mere fact of Plaid's majority must indicate a shift in public opinion in the principality. This raises an interesting question in itself: in the case of secession would the eldest son of the English monarch still be styled Prince of Wales?

It is also interesting to analyse what has brought about this first major swing towards nationalism. Clearly the reduction in the Welsh subvention, that portion of the budget voted by Westminster to sustain the Welsh economy and public services, following the collapse of London as the world's banking and financial centre, and Westminster's failure to find a replacement for it and its contribution to GB's total GDP, has had a massive knock-on impact on the local economy. Even more lost jobs have added to the already high unemployment while the downturn in the rest of the country has meant there is little to be gained from moving to London and the South East. EU regional development funds are of course no longer accessible, otherwise Wales would have been able to call on the same booster funding that has come to the rescue of Ireland and helped with Scottish infrastructure projects.

✤ ✤ ✤

'Do sit down Terry,' the Principal says, waving her into the chair opposite. She has never called Terry by her first name before but always formally: 'Dr Ellis'. It's a bad sign.

'Thank you,' Terry says, composing herself.

'I don't think this has broken in the press yet so I wanted to talk to you first. We've had a new, what shall I call it, ultimatum from the Department of Education following the minister's appointment post the election. You must understand none of this accords with my own principles or wishes. It's a dictat from on high, from those who must be obeyed. Of course it can lead, in my view, to nothing less than the impoverishment of our academic staff, the quality of research and teaching, and a loss to our students. But it seems we have no choice. I have to tell you that I have been instructed that we may no longer employ openly gay staff in educational institutions. I'm so sorry to have to tell you this.'

'I have been rather expecting something of the sort,' Terry says. 'It was really only a question of what, or how, or when. Their manifesto trailered it as part of the right-wing coalition deal. This is the soft underbelly. Abortion, under-age contraception, and the whole misogynist, pseudo-religious programme will follow. I'm afraid it's the new Clause 28, and it took more than a decade to get rid of the last one. And that was only about the equal recognition of a gay lifestyle.'

'I can only repeat how sorry I am. I have insisted that you must be allowed to serve out your contract; I suggested that the Department or the college could otherwise be sued for breach.'

'I'm grateful for your support Principal. It's a lousy thing for you to have to do.'

'You're not the only one of course. There are several more staff I have to speak to. I'm grateful that you've made it so easy for me. What will you do after this year? Go back south?'

'I've just been elected to the local council so I feel I should stay on. Discrimination hasn't been applied to local government yet. But that may not be possible.'

'No, as you say: we're the soft underbelly. You didn't find any problems standing for office?'

'It simply didn't come up. If it does I shall be quite open. I won't lie about my sexuality.'

'Tell me, from your expertise in politics, is there really no such thing as progress, the advance of progressive views?'

Terry thinks for a moment. 'There's nothing inevitable about progress even in ways of thinking. At least that's how it seems to be. Anything can be reversed. Think of the massive funding from some quarters for so-called gay cures. Or, in another area, calls to bring back the death penalty. Or the reversal of the ban on hunting. Many people thought that particular battle had been won but a powerful lobby and a less humane climate lost it again. Anything can be reversed under 'moral' pressure massively financed.'

'How depressing!'

'But there's always hope and people who will fight.'

'And you're one of them. Where do you get your energy? I'm afraid I just go limp.'

'Sheer bloody-mindedness, I expect. But you mustn't run yourself down Principal. You fought for my right to the contract. And you will for the others I know.'

'So little though. It's so little. But thank you for saying so. From my point of view you are just the sort of person I want on my staff. Your contribution while you've been here has been tremendous.'

'She was really upset,' Terry tells Jane Sims later. 'Keep it to yourself until it's official or at least until she's had time to speak to everyone involved.'

'I don't want to lose you out of the department. I wish I could think of anything I could do. It's so putting the clock back. I can't believe people really support it.'

'80 odd per cent voted to keep Clause 28 up here when the government wanted to abolish it.'

'But we've moved on since then. At least I thought we had.'

'It's just a cynical play by the extreme nationalists to stay in power by keeping the religious vote. Think of all the trouble with the church over gay marriage, and gay priests.'

'Don't! I'm depressed enough. What does Paula say?'

'I haven't had a chance to tell her yet. If it means I'm finished here at the end of my contract she may be, if not thrilled, at least relieved.'

Jane Sims gets up from behind her desk as Terry prepares to leave. Throwing her arms round Terry she says: 'I'll miss you.' It's a first for Jane, and Terry isn't sure how to respond. In the end she says nothing but puts out a hand to touch Jane's arm before turning towards the door.

'What did Jane say?' Paula asks later.

'I think she was rather upset that she couldn't do anything about it.'

'What will you do?' Terry hears Paul's carefully neutral question and sees her equally controlled expression.

'I'll see out my contract of course but there's no point in standing as a councillor now. I'll have to try for something down South. How about stacking shelves at Tesco's? Do you think they'd give me a job?'

'Leave Scotland? What about the cottage?'

'Oh we'll keep that. Who knows: the wind may change again but not till this lot has blown over. Sorry about the stormy metaphor. Only clichés seem to fit at the moment. I suppose at least I'm not being made to drink hemlock like poor old Socrates.'

Paul hears the bitterness in Terry's voice. 'Shall I come up at the weekend for a few days?'

'Could you? Only if it's okay for you.'

'I want to be with you.'

⚜ ⚜ ⚜

202?

The princess is out riding
Riding, riding.
The bad men are in hiding
Hiding, hiding.

'Mummy, I've been kidnapped!'
'Don't be silly darling.'
'But it's true.'
'And I'm the Queen of Sheba.'
'Honestly.'

Why aren't you on my screen so I can see where you are then?'

'They made me turn off the visual before they would let me call you so you couldn't see where I am.'

'So where are you?'

'I don't know. Some big house in the highlands.'

'Alright I'll go with your game. How did you get there ? And the horse? Where's that?'

'I think they put him in a stable. There were two cars and a loose box.'

'Okay. If you've been kidnapped how much do they want or do you just want me to pay off your debts?'

'It's not like that, not about money. They want me to be Queen of Scots.'

'Are the supposed 'they' listening to all this?'

'Yes.'

'So who are they?'

'They think independence hasn't gone far enough. They don't want an English king. At least that's what I understand. They want me to be called Margaret. I said I couldn't just change my name but they said royals often do. Great grandpa was really David not George at all. Is that true?'

'I seem to remember that, yes. Or was he Bertie and David was his brother, King Edward? I always found it confusing. Darling are you alright? You're not making all this up? Why were you out riding alone?'

'Oh I just wanted a gallop and nobody else did. They all had hangovers.' 'But how did the kidnappers know?'

'I asked them that but they wouldn't say. I guess it must have been someone in the house.'

'So what do they want you to do? What happens next?'

'They say they're going to take me somewhere to be crowned.'

'They'll need an archbishop for that.'

'I think they've got one.'

'Did they say where? Oh it's a horrid thing to have happened. You know someone tried it on me once. In the Mall, and my poor bodyguard was shot. They do know it won't be legal. Darling, darling are you there? The line's gone dead..!'

※ ※ ※

The first minister is in session with the Head of Security.

'I've had a call from the Palace.'

'Which one? Holyrood?'

'Buckingham.'

'Well, well.'

'I think you should show me more respect. It's still our monarch.'

'In person?'

'No. The head of security.'

'So, what's up?'

'One of the Family has been abducted.'

'Sorry but not our problem.'

'Yes it is. She's being held here. Some daftie fringe group is proposing to crown her Queen of Scots.'

'You're joking! How do we know this? It could be a hoax.'

'Unfortunately not. They allowed her to speak to her mother but not to say where she's being held or where they're taking her. Obviously we have to do something, attempt a rescue. And it had better succeed otherwise we shall look a glaikit fools. As it is we should never have let it happen. Where was intelligence? I want all the possible perpetrators investigated. And I want to know where they'll take her for this fake ceremony.'

'I can suggest a couple of places straight away: Scone or Dunkeld where Kings of Scotland were crowned in the past.'

'Is that all?'

'There's Iona but that's too full of tourists and religions. It's got to be somewhere symbolic but preferably unpopulated or at least unknown outside the history books. My money's on Dunkeld. There's the ruins of the cathedral and it's where Kenneth McAlpin made his capital and religious centre.'

'How do we do this?'

'Well it's not far from Balmoral Castle as the crow flies. If you can get permission we can put a platoon in there, ostensibly practising for a royal inspection, make it look good with pipes and parades, and put the word about. From there we can recce Dunkeld.'

'And if you're wrong and it isn't there?'

'At the same time we'll have men on exercise in the Sidlow Hills ready to descend on Scone. But my money's on Dunkeld. You get permission to send in the troops and close Balmoral to the public.'

'And you step up the intelligence. We need to know where they're taking her for sure.'

❖ ❖ ❖

The princess looks out from her castle prison across the battlements towards the Grampians, over the tops of tall trees that sail like galleons through the valleys to the River Tay. They, who ever 'they' are, are treating her well though the food is on the traditional side. She does her best with it but balked at haggis and a kind of black pudding. She longs to go riding over the hills and beside the water. Once they let her canter about a field, carefully watched by an armed, masked guard, for exercise. They tell her it won't be long now till her crowning, that she will enter the chosen place on horseback and dismount before an altar, where a throne has been placed with a replica of the Stone of Scone in its base. 'Something, the real thing, the English took from us, like so much else they haven't given back. That's why we're taking it for ourselves.'

The princess doesn't argue. Her captors never let her see their faces and although they speak politely she is aware of a constant feeling, an undertow of unease. Someone, she couldn't even be sure whether it was male or female, has measured her for her robe, and her head for, she imagines, a crown.

Then one night she is told to get a good night's sleep, that the ceremony will be tomorrow. In the morning she is urged to eat a good breakfast. Someone washes and dresses her hair. Then she is robed and given a diamond tiara to carry. She will be told when to put it on. She is led out into the drive where a closed and darkened saloon, a loosebox with its own Landover and another truck are waiting. She is handed into the black limo and the convoy sets off.

There are armed figures with her in the car, all masked by their balaclavas. Nobody speaks. Through the blacked-out windows she glimpses a high mountain. The convoy keeps up a steady forty miles an hour, then after some thirty or forty minutes comes to a stop in a clearing beside a river. The kidnappers motion her to get out. One guards her with his automatic rifle at the ready.

The back of the loosebox is opened and a handsome grey mare led out, already saddled and bridled, with silver

bells on its harness that tinkle when it shakes its head, glad
to be out of the rocking loosebox. One of her captors sig-
nals to her to put on the tiara and mount up. A kilted figure
appears from the other car and steps up to the horse's head.
The others fall in behind and the procession moves forward. The princess doesn't feel afraid, only a little excited
and unreal as if she is part of a performance, pageant or
screening.

Looking forward between the mare's white ears that
flick from time to time, picking up any strange or threatening sound, she sees that a route has been cordoned off
with signs she can't read. As they come out of the clearing
ahead of her is a ruined building, roofless, big enough to
have been some sort of cathedral. The kilted figure leads
her on through a gothic archway into the body of what must
have been the nave.

At the end a figure in priestly robes stands behind the
stone effigy of a supine knight. There is an ornate chair
placed in front of the tomb. She is helped down from the
horse and motioned forward to sit in the chair. The priestly
figure comes from behind the effigy altar, takes the tiara
from her head, turns back towards the tomb and raises
the bright chaplet in dedication. But before he can intone
any words a sudden explosion backfires into the roofless
nave. From a hidden sound system a voice booms across
the space:

'Stay exactly where you are. If you are carrying weapons
raise your hands slowly above your heads. Any false move-
ment will incur an extreme response. You are completely
surrounded and covered. We do not want bloodshed. Above
all make no attempt to seize her Royal Highness.'

For a moment the scene is frozen, then slowly arms
begin to be raised as the first troops, automatic rifles cocked,

appear silently from the archway or at the unglazed windows on either side of the ruined nave.

❧ ❧ ❧

'Thank god that's all over,' The Head of Security switches off the screen in front of them.

'Well done George. Your men did a fine job. This calls for a wee dram I think.' The First Minister goes to the drinks cabinet and fetches out a bottle and two glasses. 'Do you think we can keep it out of the media?'

'I doubt it. Someone's already blogged it. They'll allege public interest.'

'What about national security?'

'As I said. Too late. Flown the coop.'

'How do you think the public will react?'

'Someone's already started an internet poll. That should give us a steer.'

'And if it turns out that they think we should have our own queen? I wonder if she'd do it: all legal and above board this time of course?'

'You're the politician.'

❧ ❧ ❧

'Thank god you're safe darling. I had such a fright when I saw the news and realized you weren't play-acting after all. How are you feeling?'

'I'm fine Mummy. Everyone's been so nice to me. There's just one thing. They seem to want me to do it again. Only this time for real. What do you think I should say?'

'Stall them. Say you'll have to consult. We need to know what the rest of the firm thinks.'

'I wouldn't mind. I rather enjoyed it all.'

'You know what happened to the last Queen of Scots.'

'But wasn't that the English? The first Queen Lillybet? Would I be Margaret I in my own right?'

'I think so. As far as I know all the others have just been wives.'

❖   ❖   ❖

'Do you think they will vote for a Queen Margaret?' Paul asked Terry.

'Probably. There seems to be some political virus, infecting the whole world like a sort of internet borne bird flu. It attacks the host country and makes it start to fall apart into its component elements. They then get attacked in their turn into smaller and smaller fragments.'

'Was it the break up of the Soviet Union that let it loose do you think?'

'That's clever. Maybe'

'So where does it end?'

'When all the little bits have asserted their independence? Then they've got to find a way of working together.'

'But there'll always be someone who wants to be top dog, boss cat, first hen in the pecking order. It's an animal instinct.'

'I know. That's what's so depressing. We're supposed to know better.'

'So what's next for the British Isles?'

'It's already started.' Terry tossed the New Statesman across to Paul. Picking it up Paul saw among the articles trailered on the cover: New Rioting in Derry.

'Have you read it? I don't know if I can bear to.'

'Yup. Pretty depressing too. You remember not long after the beginning of the new bid for a united Ireland? Well they're making headway by driving out the Unionists who are migrating, lots of them back to Scotland or to Australia and the States.'

'So the population up here is going up.'

'And the coalition doesn't mind them coming because they were Scots in the first place or their ancestors were. In many people's eyes they're just coming home. I wish you didn't have to go back or I could come with you.'

'So do I. You know that. But I have to go and help Flora hang the next show and get my new stuff in to the RA before the deadline. We just have to hang on a bit longer till the end of term.'

'Do you get the feeling everything's falling apart around us?'

'I imagine a lot of people feel like that at the moment.'

⚜ ⚜ ⚜

Paul is walking through the city. She has been to the Barbican with some new work to display in the gallery. Kravic has remained faithful even far off in Switzerland, and comes back from time to time to view her latest pieces and take them away to be sold in Zurich or New York where he has opened a new gallery. He has plans for Frankfurt following the money, now that impoverished Englanders in Britain can no longer afford the prices of the global art market. His continued support, and the money she banks as her share for her growing international reputation he masterminds, supports her while she makes new works for places like the Barbican, and her own gallery with Flora.

'Rich buyers, they like your dark work now. I am wrong when I say before that it don't sell like your other work.'

Leaving the Barbican behind she turns into Silk Street heading South, and then down Moor Lane and East along London Wall, wondering how she can encapsulate the two thousand years of history under her feet, explicit in the street names, and the rush of buried rivers as she crosses Bishopsgate to Houndsditch and West again, glimpsing the Tower still drawing its share of tourists, the city's chief source of income.

Now she is in the deserted city, the part the tourists don't see, with its unkempt buildings and uncleaned streets. Rubbish bowls along the gutters and pavements in the currents set up by the occasional bus. The windows of the great glass steel and ceramic liners are dirty and broken. Commissioned in the boom days some were never finished, or if they were, never occupied. Paul sees an old graffito spray painted over the deserted headquarters of an international bank that London had thought would be hers forever: The Rats Have Deserted.

Some towers have been taken over as squats by the dispossessed. One, she sees, advertises a food bank in its foyer. The metal intestines lacing the Lloyds Building are streaked and pitted with rust. Although it's Wednesday lunchtime the streets, once filled at this hour with dark suited figures clutching the status briefcase and heading for the queues at the takeaways and sandwich bars, are empty. She can almost hear the ghostly tales of share deals, takeovers, futures, commodity markets, currency flows. The pink and marzipan cladding of 1 Poultry Street has crumbled from the façade in many places, leaving livid scars. A lean sliver of grey fur bunks across the road in front of her.

Across the river spires the last monument to moneyed hubris, then the tallest building in Europe, that somehow never got to look finished with its spikey shards of glass like the peaks of a jester's cap. With relief Paul sees that her namesake is unchanged, its domed breast still holding up the sky though like many of the city churches it has become a refuge for the pavvies, as those who live on the streets are called. But only the two supports on this side of the river from which the swaying millennium bridge once hung, still remain like broken teeth. First it had been made a toll crossing, so less and less used, and eventually cut up and sold for scrap.

Downhill she goes past the Law Courts, still in business, towards the Strand. And here there are more people, tourists eddying towards Trafalgar Square and eventually on to Westminster which still draws the crowds following in groups behind some banner held aloft by a tour guide determined to march them round from the genuine gothic of the abbey to the parliament fake. The whole city had become a museum, an historical monument where an empty pageant of attenuated life still lingered.

⚜ ⚜ ⚜

The committee for the Northern Federation is meeting at Boitly Hall under the wings of the Angel of the North. The Yorkshire representative, who is known for his line in gallows humour, says it's a good sign that their secret negotiations should go on in a place normally available for wedding receptions.

'Well we're discussing getting hitched aren't we?'

Some of the delegates smile. 'I think we should take this very seriously,' the Lincolnshire representative says. 'We're talking about the break-up of our country.'

'It broke up years ago. Haven't you noticed?'

'I meant England.'

'We're not breaking it; we're remaking it. As it used to be, an industrial nation. Not a metropolitan tax haven.'

'If we go on like this we'll never get anywhere.'

'We ought to elect a chair; keep us to the point.'

'Concentrated. That's it.'

'We need a strong lass, like the one who used to be a Speaker in the parliament.'

'You mean Betty Boothroyd? That was aeons ago.'

'I meant like her. No nonsense.'

'That's you missus. You're the only one present.'

'Then who'll speak up for Lancashire?'

'You'll have to get someone in for next time.'

'Right then. Any objections? No. Then we'll get started. I declare the meeting to discuss a Northern Federation with its own Assembly, similar but not identical to those of Wales, Northern Ireland and Cornwall, in session.'

'Wales is independent.'

'I speak historically. Our grounds for this are that economic strength no longer lies in the South with the service industries of finance but in the reindustrialised North of high tech SMEs and the langer steelworks and their feeders supporting the car industry. Agreed?'

'Aye, aye!' Several voices take up the call.

'So the first thing we need to settle is: who's in and who's out.'

⚜ ⚜ ⚜

Terry stepped off the ferry onto the pierside overseen by the statue of Burns' sweetheart Highland Mary, and began making her way along the walk towards the little seaside town and the cottage. Today the loch was gunmetal grey like the nuclear submarines that had once berthed there. Passing along Alexander Parade she turned down again towards the shore and the row of fishermen's cottages that had survived the brief years of its glory as a seaside resort. As she came in sight of them she saw the road was blocked with a crowd of people, police cars and two fire engines. The cottage was ablaze, smoke pluming from its windows.

Terry ran forward and began pushing her way to the front of the onlookers. A police cordon was holding back the crowd.

'Nae further Miss.'

'That's my house, the one on fire.'

'Well thank your stars ye weren't inside. Is there anyone else there? It's so fierce, the fire, that no one can get near. They're trying to get it under control before it spreads to the other cots on either side. At least we've plenty of water.'

Great arcs sprung from the steel throats of the hoses, that gleamed red where the flames caught on them as they played on the roof and windows.

'How did it start?' Terry asked.

'We'll know for sure in a day or two but to my eye, in my experience, it looks like arson. I smelt petrol when I first got here and it was first taking hold. Ye'll need to put up somewhere for the night. Ask at the tourist office on Alexander. They'll find you somewhere. There's nothing to be done here till it's under control.'

There was a curious fascination in watching the struggle between fire and water. For a time it seemed as if fire would win. But gradually water began to prevail after the roof had collapsed inwards letting the hoses play directly down into the blackening cave. When the last flame was out Terry turned away, unsure how she felt except that now she understood the sensation of numbness that had gripped Paul.

The tourist office was able to book her a room at nearby Gossops Lodge, and after a couple of drinks at the bar she found a late night superstore that conveniently sold pants and t-shirts, toothbrush and paste. Another couple of drinks and she was able to fall into a haunted sleep after texting Paul goodnight, saving the news of the fire for daylight.

'Thank god you weren't asleep inside.'

'That's what the nice copper said.'

'What will you do now?'

'Well, I'll go down this morning after I've rung Jane to let her know. I don't think the students will mind an extra morning off. I want to see what's left and figure out how to deal with the insurance without any policy document apart from a few charred bits of paper, or not even that.'

'Can't you just come home?'

'I will. As soon as I can, believe me. Thank god it's only a couple of weeks till the end of the year and my contract.'

'Come in and see me when you can,' Jane Sims said. 'Have you got somewhere to stay? If not, you're welcome to my spare room for the rest of term. I've got an extra key I can let you have. You can't be paying hotel bills.'

'Thanks Jane. That's really kind. I'll let you know how I get on. I'll have to get some more replacement kit if everything's just ashes.'

As she turned into the street she could see the loch lying sullen beyond, and the front of her cottage in the row seeming curiously unscathed at ground level, until she looked up at the second storey, roofless with blackened walls. Nearer she could see writing: a notice announcing: Dangerous Structure. Keep Out. Then lower, a defacement with black spray paint, the same words that had been scrawled on the flip chart: 'No foreign dykes here'. Only this time she couldn't turn the page.

❦   ❦   ❦

AD600

In those days when king fought against king in Hibernia an attempt was made as I have said to settle affairs between the Northern O'Neill and Dal Riata without bloodshed. But still it continued for many years, king against king, tribe against tribe, throughout all the lands of the islands, Christian and pagan. The name of that battle which Colm had prophesied as he journeyed back from the meeting of the kings with Abbot Colman, was the name of the place, Dun Cathinn, and the victor was that Conall mac Aedo whom Colm had blessed as a boy.

❦   ❦   ❦

Part Three

202?

Paul is driving North up the M1, breaking her journey at the turn off for Lincoln to spend the night and admire the cathedral, hoping its flyting columns might inspire her. She's in competition for a new commission to decorate the entrance hall to the new assembly building so the car is loaded with samples and pictures from her portfolio. If she gets this commission she will be less dependant on handouts from Kravic but it may mean moving North for a bit, just as Terry will be coming South.

'Of course you must go,' Terry had said, 'go and sock it to them, though I don't quite understand why Birtley.'

'It's got the Angel of the North.'

'So why does it need the Assembly for the Northern Federation?'

The debate had been passionate, with first one representative then another threatening to walk out. Manchester had a strong claim with its existing magnificent town hall but Liverpool, Newcastle, York and Birmingham had suggested that they should call themselves: The Federal Republic of the North.

'That's unconstitutional!'

'We don't have a constitution. Only Magna Carta.'

'It's the royal family that provides continuity.'

'Well we're against hierarchy. That's what got us into this mess: the metropolitan hierarchy of money. And anyway there's more than one head of state. Remember Scotland.'

'I don't think those I represent would want to be party to this.' The Lincolnshire delegate got to her feet.

'Do we take it then that you don't wish to be part of the federal discussion either?' the Chair asked.

'We have discussed the way things are going and we aren't comfortable with the turn of it. I have authority to withdraw.'

'You'll stick with the South then?'

'We believe that's what our constituents would wish.' She gathered up her papers and bag and headed for the door.

'You'll be back when we're successful.'

'I doubt it.'

Some delegates turned to watch her go while others stared down at their papers. The door shut with a click.

'So back to the site for the new...what should we call it: 'capital', 'parliament', 'althing'?'

'What's that?'

'That's what our Anglo-Saxon ancestors called it. I got it from a quiz show.'

'I think we should stick to 'assembly', and it should be somewhere neutral.'

'How about Birtley, where we first met? Then we get the Angel thrown in.'

Paul of course knew none of this, only that the grand new building was to be by a renowned architect and needed decorating with both murals and sculpture if it was to rival Manchester and be better than the London meeting place,

which now occupied the Queen Elizabeth Conference
Centre across Parliament Square, since the Victorian
building by Sir Gilbert Scott had fallen into terminal dis-
repair. There was even talk of taking over what had once
been the seat of London's government for the federation
of London boroughs, Old County Hall, and expelling the
hotel and aquarium it housed. The fishes would have to
swim elsewhere.

'Do you think you should try for it?' Terry had asked.

'What do you mean?'

'Isn't it a bit iffy? Encouraging more fragmentation?'

'I don't know. It might head it off if people feel they've
got a voice, aren't always under London's domination. I
think there's always been a lot of resentment of that, the
neglect of the regions, as well as of the big bits that can claim
to be independent countries like Wales and Scotland.'

'I hope you're right. I don't want us to be left with only
the shires, the home-counties, even more split between the
haves and have-nots.'

'Can you think of any other way? And anyway we need
the money.'

'I'm sorry I'm going to be a drag on you until I can find
something.'

'You're not a drag. Think how often you've had to support me. And anyway you will find something. I know you
will.'

'I've started looking but jobs are very thin on the
ground.'

That was before the fire at the cottage. After that Paul
said: 'Do you think, sometimes I think, Scotland didn't want
us.'

'That's just superstition. Some people there, who may
not even be Scots, didn't want us. That's all.'

Terry was glad to be on the train going South. Life at Jane Sims' had become increasingly tense. At first Terry had seen Jane's concern as a kind of motherliness but she had begun to feel uneasy, and that it was something other that she had never suspected. The prof had always been very circumspect in her dealings with students but Terry now felt that might merely have been a professional mask, and that Terry's physical presence in her home was causing the cover to slip. Jane had insisted on accompanying her to the station, and had flung her arms round her, and kissed her goodbye with the glitter of unshed tears in her eyes before Terry could break away.

'You know you can always come back.'

'Thanks Jane. You've been great.'

Now she could lie back in her seat and watch the countryside unravelling its tapestry of fields, chequered from time to time with black and white Friesians or splodged with the white fleeces of sheep, or glossed with shiny brown coated horses.

Paul had studied examples of the distinguished international architects' work from around the world, as well as the projected elevation the contestants for the commission had been sent. Unlike the arrogant, angular statements in glass, steel and marble whose derelict precincts she had walked through, this building was to be low and flowing, echoing the landscape around it, with the contours of a reclining nude.

Paul is on a shortlist of three. In her portfolio she has sketches for the murals, and maquettes for the sculptures she is proposing. She sits nervously in the foyer of the hotel where the interviews are being held. A door opens and a familiar figure from the media appears smiling and shaking hands with someone she recognises from the Fine Art

Department she had to leave, and all confidence drains away. The media face nods to her in passing.

'Ah, Paula, good to see you. Do come in.'

'Dick, what are you doing here?'

'I saw the writing on the wall and when a professorship came up here I applied. It's not a powerhouse like Glasgow but after all it's where it all began.'

'How do you mean?'

'The Lindisfarne Gospels: the beginning of English art.'

'Isn't art always beginning?'

'Maybe you can see it as that fluid but we have to cut it up into chunks to examine the process. Can I help you with those? I hope you're feeling better; fully recovered?'

'I hope so, though maybe it's something you never quite forget. If you could just take the portfolio I can carry the box. It isn't all that heavy.'

Now she must make her pitch.

'Perhaps you would like to look at my ideas for the murals first.'

'And when would you be free to start if you are successful Ms Sanderson?' 'As soon as the walls are ready. This is my proposal for the ceiling.'

'That's interesting. I don't think we had imagined that but, symbolically, it's important of course that people should look up as well as round, especially politicians.'

His colleagues laugh approvingly.

❧ ❧ ❧

AD 600

Now I must tell you that the whole monastery of our island was enclosed on the North, West and South by a bank and ditch against any enemies, especially from the North, but on the East side it was open down to the shore where our boats were moored. And within this bank we were like a village that grew as more came to join us, drawn by Colm's love of God, and wishing for a life dedicated not to this world of lustfulness and bloodshed but to the peace to be found in the life of the Lord. And so from time to time the bank was remade to enclose more land.

At its centre was the church where Colm was to end his mortal life. Beyond was our meeting house where he sat writing. At night he would go to his lodging where he slept, not on straw but on stone, with another for his pillow.

There was the great house for the brothers and also barns where the grain would be carried in to be stored when we had reaped it, and where it would be threshed. Also there were stables for the horses and one of these, a white one, Colm called his special friend.

Beyond the meeting house was the kitchen where we cooked our simple food, and made our barley bread and porridge. Apples and nuts were also stored in the barns and in autumn we gathered berries from the hillside and took honey from the bees. Also cattle were kept for milk and meat.

Many crosses were set up in the monastery compound, the greatest, that in remembrance of Colm himself, sat in a millstone so that the winter winds should not tear it down.

⚜   ⚜   ⚜

202?

The First Minister addresses his hastily assembled cabinet with a grave face. 'Sorry to drag you all back during recess but I didn't feel it was a decision I could take on my own. We've had a request from Ulster for help in putting down the insurgency there. Apparently England, London, won't or can't help since they ran down their army because they couldn't afford it. You'll have seen how the riots over there have escalated into something closer to civil war, a return to the Troubles, with each as bad as the other. Only this time it's both political and sectarian religious elements.'

'Hasn't it always been?'

'Yes Sandy, in a way you're right of course. But this time it's not religio-political sectarian. It's more like we had here until reason reasserted itself.'

'When was that? I must have blinked and missed it.'

'You're a cynic, Sandy. Or you forget what it was like for a time with the coalition of extreme nationalists and Christian religious right of every sect, coming on like old fashioned jihadists. That's what they're getting now.'

'So what do they want us to do?'

'Send over a battalion of troops. I suggest the Gordons. Unless you've a better idea Commander.'

'As long as nobody thinks they're the 'Gay Gordons'!' Laughter from the cabinet members. 'Certainly not the Black Watch; too reminiscent of the Black and Tans in the last century.'

'They also want me to take part in talks with the Taosearch, here or in Dublin or Stormont.'

'Our price should be independence: no union with London or Dublin.'

'I've been thinking along the lines of an extended Celtic Federation. Then we could have a treaty with the Scands for the North Sea as far as the arctic and West to Baffin Island and the Canadian territorial waters: a quarter of the northern pie.'

'Do you think they'd wear it?'

'It would solve the regions' problems.'

'A new NEU. Think of the resources it would have: A pity we didn't requisition Fasslane. Then we could have applied to join NATO as a nuclear power. I know the old government promised to get rid of them but London didn't really want them and now the subs are just mothballed there they'd be glad not to pay us the rent for the loch.'

'That's looking a long way ahead. First we have to settle Ulster.'

'I take it then I've got your say-so to go ahead with sending a peacekeeping force and opening preliminary talks.'

'Do you think they'll agree to give up the union with London?'

'They'd be better off with us. That's the more natural alignment. Those who don't like it can emigrate, if anywhere will have them.'

❧ ❧ ❧

'So how did it go?'

'Okay I think. They'll let us know who's got it next week. I wondered…even if I don't get this it's given me lots of ideas. Would you come up with me to a festival.'

'What sort of festival?'

'That's what I want to find out. We could make it a long weekend. It's ages since we've been away together.'

'Where is it exactly? It doesn't mean tents in a muddy field?'

Paul laughs. 'You're such a pioneer, you. No it's in Durham which has lots of hotels, a university and the Durham Miners' Institute where most of it will be. No muddy fields.'

So they have come to Durham where the huge stone thighs of the cathedral's twin towers stand sentinel above the city.'

'I've never been here before,' Terry says looking out from their hotel window. 'It's magnificent.'

'There's a concert tonight I rather want to go to. Shall we give it a try? It might involve a bit of muddy field?'

'Give me a kiss and I'll consider it.'

'It's part of the miners' gala.'

'Bribe me!'

The usual gaping mouth of a stage set up for open air pop concerts is open at the end of a stretch of smooth turf, with the obligatory many coloured strobe lighting, and side screens for close ups of the performers. But already the music is different. A band, the screens identify as New Northumberland Rant, occupies the stage. Smallpipes, accordion, concertina, fiddles, even a mandolin and mouthorgan jig through a series of tunes to the audience's clapped percussion: <u>Durham Rangers, Hesleyside Reel, Lassies, Marry me Now, the Wandering Tinker,</u> ending with a burst of <u>The Keel Row</u> that has the clappers stamping their feet in time.

The band put down their instruments and the spotlight picks up a lone figure coming forward to stand at the front of the stage. An announcer's voice comes over the loud-speaker system: 'Ladies and Gentlemen, Willy Barnes with the Durham Lockout!' The figure begins to sing.

In wor Durham County I'm sorry to say
That hunger and starvation are increasin' every day.
For the want of food an' coals we know not what te do,
But with your kind assistance we'll see the battle through.

I need not state the reason why we've been browt se low.
The masters have behaved unkind as everyone will know,
Because we won't lie doon and let them treat us as they
like,
To punish us they've stopped the pits an' caused the present
strike.

Well let them stand or let them lie or do whatever they
choose,
To give them thirteen and a half we ever shall refuse,
They're always willing to receive but not inclined to give,
An' very soon they won't allow a working' man te live.

There's a great crash of applause, of shouting, and
stamping which makes a muffled drumbeat on the grassy
ground. The announcer's voice comes over the applause
again: 'Not much changes, eh folks?' The band breaks into
another reel, before the disc jockey's voice announces: 'The
Weavers' March or Frisky Jenny,' as they go into the next
tune, and then the band falls silent for another singer and
The Poor Cotton Wayver.

At the end the voice says: 'That was after Waterloo
friends, when wages were low, unemployment and prices
high. Well some of us think we've met our Waterloo again.
Now altogether for The Blackleg Miner. The words are on
your screens.'

The band strikes up; a chorus comes on stage to lead
the singing:
'It's in the evening after dark,
When the blackleg miner creeps to work,
With his moleskin pants and dirty shirt,
There goes the blackleg miner.'

Paul is snapping the stage, the performers, the choiring audience. Terry glances around at the intent, open-mouthed faces. 'Look, isn't that Bob Stiles?'

'You should know baby.'

Stiles is a little way from them on a slight arc. Terry waves, and again, at last catching his eye. He waves back. Then raises an open hand to his lips making the gesture that translates· 'Shall we have a drink.'

Terry gives him the thumbs up. 'It is Bob. He wants us to have a drink.'

'Great.'

The concert draws to an end, with a young Scots singer performing the old Annie Briggs favourite, <u>The Doffing Mistress</u> , with its dash of early feminism.

Oh do you know her or do you not,
This new doffing mistress we have got?
Elsie Thompson it is her name,
And she helps her doffers on every frame.

The audience joins in, but softly now:

With me 'Ri fol dol; with me ri fol dee.'

Sometimes the boss he looks in the door,
'Tie your ends up doffers,' he will roar.
Tie our ends up we surely do,
But for Elsie Thompson and not for you.

The song unwinds like the thread from a spindle as she weaves together words and music. And where before there had been the dark of the mine, spotlit by the miners' lamps, and the clang of pick and shovel, now there's the clatter of looms, bobbin and shuttle, the air misted with flying fibres and the voices of women, having a crack or singing together, as the webs of cloth and the day lengthen.

When it's all over Paul and Terry make their way towards Bob Stiles while he pushes towards them through the murmuring crowd.

'Well, that was quite something.'

'It certainly was. Where shall we go?'

'There's plenty of pubs in Durham. That's one thing they're not short of.' He leads the way into the street. 'That looks fairly quiet. Let's try that one. My round. What would you both like?'

When they're all seated with glasses in front of them Terry says: 'You remember Paula, Bob?'

'Of course. Good to see you again but what are you both doing up here?'

'I'm doing research for a possible project.' Paul says.

'And I'm along for the ride. What about you?'

'Showing solidarity. Ever since Ed Miliband revived the tradition of the party leader speaking at the gala we've had a presence here and I like to be part of that. And I always go to the concert if there is one. I used to sing a bit myself till I got caught up in politics. What about you Terry? I thought you were in Scotland somewhere.'

'We were until things got rather hairy with the extremist right-wing grouping. Paula was caught up in a bombing and I lost my job and the cottage. So we're both back here. But who knows for how long. Is it true things are going the same way here?'

'The English Alliance, equally right-wing coalition, you mean? 'Fraid so. They're not violent, at least not overtly so, yet, but if they lose the election who knows.

At the moment it's just a general oppressiveness towards minorities of all sorts. What are you doing about a job? Could you be persuaded to come back? You know there's a rumour that this part of the country wants its own version of independence. And I can understand it. The songs you heard appeal again because people see now reflected in them.'

'History as myth and just as powerful.'

'As I seem to remember you saying.'

'It didn't do me any good but I still believe it.'

'What did you have in mind for Terry, Bob?'

'Standing at the next election.'

'Wouldn't there have to be a selection process? She might not get through it. Then where would she be?'

'Oh I'd make sure she had every support. We need more women. We always do.'

'But meantime while she's waiting?'

'I can sign up for some supply teaching or look for part time that I can get out of if I'm elected.'

Paul laughed. 'I can see you're hooked again. I'd better get that commission.'

'Can I ask what it's for?' Bob said.

'It's for the new Northern Assembly, if I get it.'

❧   ❧   ❧

'Will you come and see me in Portcullis House,' Bob Stiles had said, 'when we're both back.'

So Terry is taking up his invitation. Passing Boudicca at full gallop beside Westminster Bridge, where a few tourists still linger looking for past glories in their guide books, she thinks: One day I'd like my photo taken hanging on to your chariot up there.

Then she turns in at the revolving door. She still has her MP's pass, and is waved through into the atrium where the light now filters through the curtain of grime, veiling the glass roof. The huge space, once bustling with its café at the far end, and dotted with figures passing importantly through or in small groups in conversation with the con-stituents and lobbyists hawking their ideological or financial goods, is now so unnervingly empty that Terry's relieved to see Bob Stiles waving at her across the central island where stumps and trunks of dead trees lie where they have fallen.

'What happened?' Terry asks gesturing at the downed carcasses of the trees.

'I think we ran out of money to pay someone to water them. We're treating it as conceptual art, a symbol of the times, reminding us of what we've lost. Though I can't say I weep over some of the 650 members there used to be.'

'So now how many are there?'

'It's down to 350. And if Cornwall follows Wales there'll be even fewer.'

'I'd forgotten about the Welsh. That comes of keeping my head down in academe. There things move at a different pace. Here they've been hurtling along.'

'It's the domino effect. One goes and the others begin to think what's good for them may be good for us.'

'Meanwhile Scotland gets stronger with the setting up of the Celtic Federation.'

'I tell you what: I expect the two Irelands to join.'

'Both?'

'Think about it. I'll get us something to drink. I rec-ommend coffee. The tea's a bit weak. 'Gnat's pee,' my mother would have called it. So,' Bob says when he's set down the two cups and two small packets of custard creams. 'Can I tempt you?'

'How would it work now?'

'I'll have a word in various ears and sound out the party leader. You come to the party conference.'

'How do I do that?'

'I'll get you a ticket as an expert on higher education. We'll have a fringe meeting you can speak at on some related topic. We can work all this out more fully later if you're willing to give it a go.'

'Bob, why are you so keen on getting me back?'

'Because we need new blood. I've heard you speak. You're good. We need that. With a big push we might get back next time. And you know something about how this place works but more importantly you know the world beyond the Westminster village. And we need that too, not to be accused of being out of touch like the other lot.'

'But where would I stand? Isn't everyone hanging on to their seats?'

'Well, it so happens that there's something coming up in your neck of the woods. Joe Stevens is standing down for South East London, Camberwell division. Isn't that where you live?'

⚜ ⚜ ⚜

'I love the colour of your skin,' Terry says stroking Paul's bare shoulder.

⚜ ⚜ ⚜

Paul is flying from Hub Northolt with its complex of runways and airport buildings that had succeeded in covering RAF Northolt and its surrounding golf course, playing fields and recreation ground, in a concrete and Tarmac web, and engulfed a section of Western Avenue. She is off to Geneva where Kravic has demanded her presence at the opening of his next show. Knowing that once the Assembly commission is all finished she will need his support again, and the underpinning income it brings in, she has agreed to go although she hates flying and is unhappy, disorientated by the vastness of airports, especially she fears this one: the most extensive in the western world after John F Kennedy.

To make it easier Terry drives her across London through empty city streets from Southeast to Northwest and parks the car in the vast hangar of indoor car park with its scatter of occupied places. Then the ritual of check in, a last cup of coffee together and a goodbye hug. Paul turns to wave bravely as she carries her bag through the departure turnstile. Few travellers follow her. The giant hub, built to bolster the return of vanished money, now worked at a mere fifty per cent capacity since London was no longer finance capital of the world. Now it wasn't even Orwell's vision of Airship One, Oceania since the new aircraft could fly direct across the world without changing airlines and the few tourists whose curiosity brought them to the city to inhale its whiff of Gotterdammerung, could hop across the channel or burrow under it in innumerable ways, to land directly at Stratford for the precariously surviving annual Shakespeare festival, or Balmoral for the Highland Games in the presence of Scotland's reigning monarch. At such times the air buzzed with clouds of short haul craft droning towards their destinations.

⚜ ⚜ ⚜

'Why do I do this? Why did I agree to come? I have nothing in common with these people. To them I'm just an exotic curiosity. They're barely looking at the work. Yet they'll buy it almost sight unseen to be seen themselves, the price is that of their status not that of the picture. I know Terry would say I'm too hard on them, that they're only human but they corrupt everything they touch. It turns to lead not gold and the only value of that is what it sells for.

The women are all dressed as if for a film premiere. The men too, mostly suited with here and there an Armani leisure throw-away downdresser. All tanned, coiffed, jewelled. And the streets are the same, filled with glossy boys and girls with smooth golden skin heading for the lake and the garden restaurants beside it, to gaze out over the crammed marina's sailboats as they knock against each other when a steamer sets up the turbulence of its wake.

I told Kravic I couldn't work here and it's true; so absolutely true. I can already feel a kind of numbness creeping over me; the mind and eye going dead like the dulling eye of a landed fish. There are no poor, no brown or black faces on these streets. The culture of comfort, homogenised, safe, doesn't allow for difference.

Maybe outside the city it's different, where people are mixed with other breathing, shitting creatures with their furry hides and horny feet. Maybe there's more sense of warm humankind. Or maybe the whole place is a bubble insulated from reality. No, I was right; I couldn't work here.

If he asks me again I can plead the commission. I must try to circulate. He's bringing an elderly woman towards me, a double row of pearls lying in the folds of her neck. Would she let me paint her just like that, as I see her? Would I when I'm her age?

'Cara, let me introduce the Contessa D'Albina.'

'Madame.'

'You are very clever girl no. Devo avare one of your pictures. Maybe you paint me. Yes?'

'Madame I would be honoured but I'm afraid I don't do portraits.'

'You do him.' She is pointing with an ornate cane at the picture of the Mexican sweeper.

'He was just an ordinary person. His work interested me, the leaves and the brush.' I'm lying but not completely.

'You will think about it. I want the best. If Kiril think you are good, show your pictures, va bene per me. E abbastanza.'

'I promise I will think about it.' She's holding onto my arm with surprisingly strong, heavily be-ringed fingers. I want to knock her hand away as I would an insect that's settled on me but I know I mustn't. Why do I find her so repellent? Think Paul. Be honest with yourself. Is it because that's what lies in wait for all of us? Is it my own decay and mortality? She can't help being old, a survivor, with a tenacity that's admirable in its way. So what's with you? Is it the rings, the assumption she can buy it? The stink of money. Hold a copper coin too long as you did as a kid when pennies meant something and your hand will smell of sweaty metal.

'Excuse me. I have to speak to someone over there.'

'Va bene. I speak to Kiril for my picture.'

❧ ❧ ❧

Terry is turning out books to go to the charity shop and make room on the shelves for new ones when she comes across a battered atlas, so old it must have been her mother's, and indeed as she pulls it off the shelf, it falls open at the first page and there's her mother's maiden name in the top right hand corner. Flicking the title pages over she sees that it's even older than her mother would have been, printed before the Second World War when the world in Mercator's projection looked very different. Where now it's many coloured by its diffuse nationalisms then, apart from the blocks of America and Russia, it was patched all over with empire red. Now, she thought, there would be just one blob from the channel to Berwick and, Clacton to Hereford or Hull to Liverpool, wherever you took the measure, and even that was paling the further North you went into a dusty pink within the border of black, green or blue.

She had to make her final speech of the campaign that evening, words that would stir the audience to get the vote out. Apathy was the real enemy, the feeling, that for some became an article of faith, that there was nothing to be done, that the politicians once elected were all corrupted by power and would do whatever suited them. And weren't the parties themselves just another form of tribalism: one group of baboons seeing off another.

'What's worrying you?' Paul asked. 'I know that look.'

'Suddenly I don't know if I can do it, if I even want to.'

'Of course you can and do. It's just first night nerves. What's that old book you're holding?'

'It's an atlas that must have been my mother's or even someone before her. Look that's what the world looked like then: the British Empire. Except that it wasn't really British, it was English. That's why all the foreign languages call it some form of England: Angleterre, Ingilterra; you know.'

'Do you think the Romans made a better job of loss of empire?'

'They got a second holy one for a time. But at least Italy's managed to stay in one piece so far. We're like Humpty Dumpty.'

'So somebody's got to try to stick us together again.'

The big room in the upstairs of the library is packed. 'Go and sock it to them. I'll try to sit at the back,' Paul said.

Terry makes her way to the front where there's a table used by the librarian on duty and raised a step above the rest of the room, two chairs and a lectern. The book lined walls slightly muffle the sound. Quickly she decides not to use the lectern. Other tables have been pushed to the sides and the space filled with chairs. The acoustic will be very dead. She will have to raise her voice. As always on these occasions she wishes she were taller.

'All set?' the chairman says, shaking her hand.

'I hope so.'

'I'll just introduce you and then they're all yours. Just let a few more in though they'll have to stand. Good turnout at least. Lot of young people. You should play well with them.' He sits down and waves Terry into the other chair. There's an unnerving pause while more people shuffle in, some to sit on the floor, others to lean against the bookstacks. 'Are you using the lectern,' the chairman whispers.

'No,'

'Good. I won't then. I always think it looks less formal, less like a lecture. Okay, shall we go? I'll get the doors shut and we can get started.'

Terry doesn't hear his introduction because of the silent drumming in her ears, only the muted applause at the end. The chairman turns towards her and sits down. She stands up and goes round to the front of the table, 'Good evening ladies and gentlemen, and anyone who isn't. Thank you for coming out this evening.'

There's a ripple of laughter. 'As you all know I'm here to try to persuade you to vote for me, and I want to begin by setting out what I believe has happened to us, and then what I think needs to be done for us to find ourselves again. Because I believe that in the last decade or so we've lost our way and have been conned into becoming a less caring, a more self-centred society. And I don't believe that's our natural way of being, or even in our so-called interest. Friends, we can do better than that; we are better than that.' Someone begins to clap and then others join in with a few accompanying whistles and 'here, heres' from older people, mostly party officials, sitting in the front row.

'Well done,' Paul says when it's all over, the applause finally dies away and people begin getting to their feet and turning to talk to each other. 'You got them. You really got them.'

The chairman shakes her hand. 'I think we've got ourselves a winning candidate. Congratulations. Now it's up to us all to go on the stump and make sure they all vote.'

Over at a side table volunteers were signing up to help, leafleting, emailing, providing transport for those who still preferred the ballot box to the computer. 'I'll just have a word with the secretary's, Liz's lot, and then I expect you could do with a drink. I know I could.' He hurried away.

'Sorry about this but I suppose we have to.'

'Lie back and think of England.'

⚜ ⚜ ⚜

AD 600

Although Colm had not wished to crown Aedan mac Gabrain King of Dal Riata yet when he was ordered to do so by God's angel with the glass book he obeyed and after was ready to give him his blessing, and predict what would befall him. King Aedan was involved in many battles and, before one of them against the barbarian Miathi near their fortress of Dunmyat, he came to ask Colm which of his three eldest sons would succeed him: Artuir, Eochaid Find or Domangart. Then Colm said: 'None of them, for all three will die in battle, but let your younger sons come in and God's chosen one will run to me.' They were then called in and Eochaid Buide went straight to Colm and laid his head on Colm's breast. Colm kissed and blessed him and told his father that this was the son, and his sons after, that would succeed him.

Not long after, as I have said, King Aedan fought against the barbarians of the North but although he was victorious Artuir and Eochaid Find, his sons, were killed. Although their brother Domangart survived it was not to be for long as he too was killed, leading his father's army with the Britons against the Saxons.

Marginal gloss in a later hand.

This King Aidan was later defeated by Aethelfrith, King of the English, at the battle of Degsa's Stone together with many Britons and great slaughter so that Aidan was forced to flee with the few that were left, and after that no King of the Scotti in Britain has dared to fight against the English whom God allowed to conquer them, and the Britons, because they had not brought them into the true faith, for Aethelfrith and the Saxons were still at that time in pagan darkness.

⚜ ⚜ ⚜

202?

'Suppose, just suppose you don't get it?'

'Then I'll have made a complete dog's breakfast because it's one of the safest seats in the South. But if I make a complete cock-up I can keep on supply teaching while I apply for permanent jobs. But now there's this unholy right-wing alliance I think it's even less likely. Too many people are the children or now grandchildren of emigrants to fall for that stuff.'

'But what about Europe? How do most people feel about going back in?'

'I know that's the opposition's strongest card but it's up to us, to me, to show people that coming out hasn't made us stronger. Europe's picked up. It's still our biggest market, and the bankers soon discovered London wasn't such rich pickings when it hadn't got European financial clout but that it had all gone to Frankfurt and Geneva with Kravic. I'm glad he isn't still around trying to come onto you.'

'The money was useful.'

'I know. But you don't need him now. When do you have to go back to Gateshead?'

'I should have the sketches all done by Tuesday. That's when I'm due to go up and show them to the committee. What about you?'

'I'm going canvassing on the Rye Lane Estate tomorrow.'

'You will be careful.'

'Don't worry I'll have someone with me. And anyway it's a lot better since the council revamp. So let's not worry about it now.'

'I wish you weren't going to the estate,' Paul said next morning.

'I have to. Everyone there has a valuable vote I need. And anyway they have the right to be canvassed like anyone else.'

'I know. But I'm allowed to be worried.'

'We're going in the party van and there'll be a whole group of us knocking on doors.'

But at first as they bumped off the road over the low ramp between the railings that separated the blocks of flats, sectioned by terraces of small houses, some with tended post-card sized front gardens, others with dumped and mouldering furniture or a dwarf forest of the ranker weeds, there seemed no one to accost. The van pulled up on a wide street, that led into a central low maintenance garden area of grass fringed with shrubs and hybrid tea rose bushes, between two tall gaunt blocks.

'Barley and oats,' Terry said looking at the map on her mobile. 'Which shall we do first? Start at the top and wok our way down?'

'Alphabetical: Barley,' the local secretary said. 'What do you bet the lift isn't working.'

'Okay. Off we go.'

A ragged curtain twitched at a ground floor window as they moved towards the columned entrance. A face appeared for a fleeting moment and was withdrawn too fast to say if it was man or woman.

'I expect they think we're the police,' Terry thought. 'Even though the van says: Vote Labour. It could be just a trap. Glancing to her left towards the garden she saw a little group of three men who had been smoking unnoticed under the arch of a stairway, dissolve and move away in different directions.

The lift stank stalely and although there was a no-smoking notice old butts littered the floor. At least it was working. They stepped out onto the top walkway, glad of the fresh air until a gust of wind bowled a collection of dust and litter around them.

Phil, the treasurer knocked on the first door. There was no reply. They waited, already a little chilled by the greyness of the stretch of concrete balcony with its chipped railings.

'I thought this place had been refurbished. Give it another try Phil. Then we'll move on.'

'So did I.' Once again he knocked on the door which kept its blank face turned unanswering towards them.

'Try the bell.'

'I did. It doesn't work.'

'Okay. Let's move on.'

At the third door they heard a tremulous voice in answer to their knock. 'Just a minute.' Then the sound of a bolt, a lock turning, the rattle of a chain, a face.

'Who are you? I thought you was the dinner or the carer.'

'Good morning Mrs Willoughby. I'm Terry, your candidate in the election. I hope you're going to vote for me.'

'How do I know who you is?'

'Please open the door so we can have a chat.'

'You going to make things better?'

'I want to try. I promise I'll try.'

'Promises is like piecrust, made to be broken.'

Terry laughed. 'My nan used to say that.'

There was the sound of the chain being drawn along its metal groove and the door was opened. The small figure was hardly more substantial than the shiny frame that held her up.

'You won't let them take me away. I can manage, with the dinners. The mash and that sponge pudding, they're very nice. I can eat those. And then I dip my biscuits in the tea.'

'Do your family visit Mrs Willoughby?'

'They took the boy away. He got inter bad company here. When he come out he got a job up North somewhere. There's jobs there now. Not like here. He learned something to do with little machines inside. Nannies he said they

169

were. Like your nan.' A sudden laugh showed the toothfree gums behind the sunken brown lips and cheeks.

'That's good that he got a job. Would you like a trip out to the polling station?'

'That's at St John's. I know that. Would it be in a car?'

'Of course.'

'I'll see how I feel on the day.'

'Thank you. We'll come and ask you. Anyway: here's my card. If you have any problems let me know and I'll do what I can.'

The door is closing, the bolt and chain shot into place. They move on. Telling Paul about it later Terry says: 'And I suddenly thought about her name, the name of a slave owner who got one of his slaves pregnant, as they did, so that one of the English aristocracy's classiest names ends up in Barley House on the Rye Estate. There's a sort of justice in her free meals and carers. I suppose that's why I go on. Or one of the reasons.'

Slowly they worked their way along, and then from floor to floor. Many doors remained unopened, knocks and rings unanswered. Terry hoped it meant the occupants were at work rather than lying dead, unmissed, inside. One door was opened by a young mother with sallow face and the unwashed hair of the depressed or overburdened, a baby slung in one arm, a large eyed toddler clinging to the other hand. 'I thought you was the social.'

'You're expecting them?'

'They said they was coming this morning. I don't care. They can't do nothing. As long as they don't take the kids away. I can look after them. Look I don't smoke no more.'

Terry found herself repeating the words she had used to Mrs Willoughby, offering transport, help.

'You got kids?'

'No, no I haven't.'

'So what do you know. Worst thing I ever done, have another one. But that don't mean I don't love'em and look after'em best I can. When they goes to school I'll go back to work. I used to work. As long as I don't fall again. But I won't be sterilized and he won't have the snip. I think they make holes in the johnnies deliberate, the Catholics and that, in the factories.'

It seemed as if now she had an audience the flood of misery couldn't stop.

'We've got some vouchers Mrs Evans. Local businesses who take part in our scheme to give people a few extras they might not be able to afford.'

'Oh yeah. Like what?'

'Well apart from food, there's money off for children's clothing and shoes, bedclothes, a trip to the hair dresser's…'

'I'd like that. Get me hair done proper. I never get time at home.'

'And there's a crèche where the children can be looked after while you're having your hair fixed.'

'Would it include colouring?'

'Anything you like. It's up to you. There's just one thing: they like to take your photo. Publicity.'

'Red. I've always wanted to be a redhead. I don't care about the photo. It's like them programmes on the telly where they show you before and after. Little kids with split lips getting mended! Here, I've never voted but you're not half bad. I might vote for you.'

'Thanks we'll put you down for a lift. And here's my leaflet. And Rob will give you the vouchers. I think you have to make an appointment for the hairdresser.'

'Oh I can do that. I've got me mob. I'm not stupid, you know. You can't just walk in. You always have to make an appointment.'

Terry watched as Rob shelled out a clutch of vouchers. 'Ta.' The door was slammed to. Terry turned away feeling a black damp of despair rising inside. 'It shouldn't be like this. Not now. Not ever.'

⚜ ⚜ ⚜

This time Paul's meeting is in the Old Town Hall at Gateshead, a handsome municipal building in the Northern nineteenth century tradition, a miniature castle crossed with a cathedral, now appropriately an arts centre. She has come up a day early to see again the site of the new assembly, and finds it has moved on a lot since her first visit. Now the shell of a building undulates across a field beside the A1. A bus runs close for tourists who want to see the giant figure of the Angel of the North other than glimpsed through a fast moving train window.

Paul walks back in the shadow of the sculpture towards the nascent building. A skyraking crane ferries materials to the level of the flowing ripple of the roof. Men and a few women in hard hats and orange overalls are coming and going across the site while Paul videos their movements, crisscrossing each other, behind the wheel of a blue dumper truck, or shovelling sand and cement into a churning concrete mixer. She pans across the scene, pausing from time to time for a longer focus on a particular group, a trio studying a site plan, a half dozen surrounding someone who is explaining something, sculpted against the pale ground of the curtain walls.

'Stanley Spencer's Riveters,' she thinks, feeling the excited flush of the moment of conception, knowing she will use this scene though she doesn't yet know how. Eventually she turns away to photograph the surrounding area of hills, trees and grass before heading back to the bus stand. Back at her hotel she converts some of the images still imprinted on her internal vision, with the help of the pictures she's taken, into sketches. Somehow the builders have to be on the inside for everyone to see, as well as implicit in the fabric of the building. 'Will the committee understand?' she wonders. 'And will I be able to recapture it in the cold light of tomorrow morning?'

'That's a great idea. What would you think of an accompanying video of the construction in progress concentrating on the workforce as you have? Or would that interfere with your conception?'

'That's a great idea too. I'd go along with that. It makes them actors in their own drama, as well in their portraits by me. You can have the footage I took yesterday.'

'Could you come up and brief a team?'

'Of course.'

'We're going to ask the Queen to open it.'

'I could have asked which one,' Paul said to Terry later when she was home again. 'But I thought I'd better not. Anyway I've signed the contract. I didn't really believe it until I went and saw the building actually taking shape. This gets me off the hook with Kravic. And who knows what it might lead to.'

'It'll be a lot of work won't it? Will you have to spend masses of time up there?'

'A fair bit of course. But now I know what I'm doing it'll be easier. I can't decide whether or not to just blast my way through, weekends and all, or to take it slowly, having breaks. I'll only know that when I start. Enough of me. What's next for you?'

'Well I've been selected so it's just more of the same: on the stump till the election. Fingers crossed.'

'Fingers crossed. I should get my first cheque in a few days. They're paying me in instalments, to make sure I keep to the contract I suppose. Let's celebrate. Let's go out and eat. We might as well enjoy it while we can. For both of us.'

⚜ ⚜ ⚜

Election day dawns damp and grey. Paul hopes it isn't an omen though she keeps this thought to herself. Terry almost feels she no longer cares. Exhausted she's nearly beyond feeling. It's always been a safe seat. She should win it or rather the party should but if she fails she's responsible; she hasn't worked hard enough, was the wrong candidate...All her fault, her fault. Wearily she drags herself to local party office for the last minute push to get the voters out. Volunteers are already arranging lifts, taking calls.

It's been a dirty campaign against them. Terry had forbidden personal attacks on rival candidates but the usual mudslinging had come from the main opposition, EAP, the English Alliance Party, hinting with sideways swipes at her sexuality and her lack of support for the indigenous 'English'. 'Flat-earthers who won't admit we all came out of Africa.'

Paul laughed. 'I wouldn't make that a key point in your speech. Most people won't understand it or, if they do, they'll resent it, and you. I'm afraid I'm a drag on you.'

'You're what fucking keeps me going, keeps me sane.'

Bob Stiles, now party leader, had come down to share the stump early in the campaign. 'I'm glad you agreed to come back to us Terry. We need what you bring to the CDP.'

'You know what they call us: the Communist Destroying Party.'

'I've heard worse than that.'

'It took time to count the big constituency electorate with its over fifty thousand voters, even with so much of it now done electronically. At last the returning officer signalled that he was ready. Terry texted Paul to let her know they were on their way and she should set out for the town hall.

'Thank you all. I hope we've done enough. If not it's my fault not yours. Now let's get down there. I couldn't have had a better team.' There was a round of applause from the volunteers and party activists. Then they headed towards the door, carrying Terry along in their midst on what they hoped was a wave bearing her towards Westminster.

At the top of the Town Hall steps they separated; her supporters to go to the main hall; Terry and her agent, Amina Chakraborty, to the mayor's parlour where the other candidates and their agents have nervously assembled, waiting for the mayor, the returning officer, to put them out of their misery so that they can face the waiting world with a few moments to recover and digest their fate.

By the time Paul arrives the big hall is already crowded but she manages to work her way forward through the hum of speculation. Then there's a moment's silence as a door to the left of the stage opens and, lead by the mayor, the candidates and their agents file in to climb the steps onto the stage as applause, punctuated with shouts and whistles, breaks out. Trying to guess the result from the line of faces Paul is concentrating so hard that she misses the mayor's announcement of the actual figures, until the roar from the onlookers wakes her, as if from a self induced trance, to hear him say: 'And so I declare Dr Terry Ellis duly elected.'

Terry shakes hands with the mayor and the other candidates, and then steps forward for the traditional vote of thanks to the returning officer and his team of tellers. As she speaks there is silence in the hall while the different parties come to terms with their results, positions maintained or enhanced, and for some lost deposits. Then suddenly as she is still speaking there's a shout.

'Fucking cretins you've put a fucking dyke in who likes a touch of the tarbrush.'

There are cries of 'shame', 'fuck off', 'put him out!' The mayor steps forward. 'Stewards, remove that person.'

There's a scuffle as the stewards close in. Then the man shouts: 'I'm going. This place stinks of lesbo cunt.'

Again there are cries of 'shame', whistles, that may be in support or against, as he is hustled away.

Sickened Paul doesn't know how to react. Should she hurry away, lose herself in the crowd so as not to embarrass Terry or go forward to join her? There'll be a celebration at the party offices. Should she go or just turn away for home on her own?

Suddenly through a divide in the press Terry appears. 'Come on baby,' she says throwing her arms round Paul. 'Let's party.'

⁜ ⁜ ⁜

AD 600

The time came when the four years God had ordained for Colm to continue his life in his earthly body were nearly

up. He was now much bowed by age and was drawn in a
cart when he wished to visit any part of the island. So it
happened that in the month of May he was driven to the
west of Hy where the brothers were working. Then he
began to say to them: 'Last month in April I wanted to end
my journey here and God would have let me but I put it
off a little longer so as not to spoil the joy of Easter for you
with sorrow.'

Seeing how upset they were by his words he tried to
comfort them and sitting in the cart he blessed both the
island and the islanders, before he was carried back to the
monastery. And from that day to this no viper has been able
to harm man or beast on Hy with its venomous three-forked
tongue.

The following Sunday while mass was being celebrated
as usual, his face was suddenly lit up by a glowing light as
the sky at sunset, and when the brothers asked him the reason for his shining expression of joy he answered that he
had seen an angel of the Lord flying above the altar who
was sent to tell him that the longed for hour had nearly
come and the loan was soon to be recovered by God. But
no one then understood what this loan might be that Colm
spoke of.

The following Sunday Colm and his constant attendant Diarmit went to bless the newest barn now full with two
heaps of winnowed grain. As he blessed it Colm said how
glad he was that, if he had to go away somewhere, the brothers would not go hungry. Then Diarmit said that his constant talk of going away was making them all sad.

'Then I will tell you a secret if you will promise not to
disclose it to anyone.'

On his knees Diarmit promised, and Colm went on to
say that God had revealed to him that he would die that very

day at midnight. At this Diarmit wept bitterly while Colm tried to comfort him.

Leaving the barn they climbed a little hill overlooking the monastery and stood for a while looking down at it. Then Colm prophesied that Hy would be honoured in time to come by the Kings of Scotia and other lords and peoples and that the holy men of other churches would revere it too. Then he returned to the monastery, and in his hut he returned to the copy he was making of the psalms. At the thirty fourth psalm he rested his pen at the end of the page and said: 'Let Baithene finish the rest.' After this he went to the church for vespers and then returned to his lodging to rest on his bed.

When the bell rang for matins at midnight he got up quickly and went to the church again, ahead of the others. Diarmit following close behind saw a great light suffusing the building which vanished as he reached the door.

'Father where are you?' he called out in the darkness. Feeling his way to the altar he found Colm collapsed in front of it. Sitting down beside him he raised Colm's head and cradled it on his breast as the other monks began to arrive with their lamps. At that Colm opened his eyes and looked about him with a radiant smile of joy.

Although he could not speak, as he lay dying Diarmit was able to raise Colm's right hand which he moved gently to bless the brothers. Then his head fell back against Diarmit's breast. So our beloved master passed from this earthly life to his longed-for home with the same expression of heavenly joy still lighting up his face.

Then the morning hymns were sung and Colm's body was carried back to his lodging, which he had so recently left, to the singing of the psalms by the brothers. The funeral rites appropriate to one of his birth and status, for he could have been king among our people if he had not chosen to follow a greater calling in the service of the Lord, were fulfilled, lasting three days and three nights. Then his body was shrouded in linen, and he was buried in his grave to rise triumphant on the last day. During all this time, from the moment of his passing a great tempest of wind and rain raged, so that no one could cross the Sound to Hy and only his monks were there to lay him to rest. But no sooner had they done so then the storm ceased and all was calm.

Then I determined to return to Hibernia along with Diarmit, so heavy were our hearts, and to seek comfort in his monastery of Durrow where I, now an old man, write these words so that all men who come after may know how great he was.

Amen

❧ ❧ ❧

202?

The Council to Determine the Royal Succession is meeting at the old College of Arms building in Queen Victoria Street, under the chairmanship of the Earl Marshall.

'They've asked for an observer from both Houses,' Bob Stiles had told Terry. 'I wondered if you'd represent the Commons. With your background you'll understand better than some of us what's going on. How are you getting on with the networks by the way?'

'Well I do my weekly blog and Paula vets the answers for me. She tells me anything she thinks I ought to know.'

'She protects you from hatemail. Good. Let me have your thoughts on this, though I suspect they've already got it sorted.'

So Terry found herself making her way from Mansion House, now a hotel, to the modest but charming buildings where the College still hung on to a touch of seventeenth century elegance. Passing through the high iron gates she went up the steps to be met by a figure in kneebreeches, white stockings and green silk tunic.

'I'm here for the Council meeting.'

'This way please. It's in the Earl Marshall's Court. There is tea and coffee.'

Terry found a seat at the back of the heavily panelled room, facing a railed area where sat an array of dignitaries some in clothing she had only seen in costume dramas, or when the Black Rod led the procession to the Lords for a State Opening. The figure in the middle stood up. 'Garter King of Arms,' someone announced.

'Good morning everyone. I'm afraid the Earl Marshall couldn't be present so he's asked me to take his place. I'm sure you'll be pleased to hear that their majesties have come up with an excellent suggestion that we all feel might solve our dilemma.

'Their suggestion is that since they have been blessed with twin girls that one should be Queen of England and the other Queen of the Celtic Federation.'

There was a moment's silence. Then the Scottish representative, identifiable by his accent, kilt and Tartan tie asked: 'So who gets which. Jane or Kate?'

'They could toss for it,' someone said.

'Anyway Robbie, you can't object. They both went to Gordonstown.'

'Aye and there were some strange rumours about Jane, that she was much too friendly with a royal lassie from Spain.'

'That's okay Robbie.'

'But what about the succession?'

'There's always stemcells or IVF.'

'Or another Virgin Queen. The last one didn't do too badly.'

'Order, order. Ladies and gentlemen please!'

⚜ ⚜ ⚜

Part Four

202?

'So it's up to us to decide, then?'

'You can have England, I'll have Scotland.'

'That's not fair. I'd rather have Scotland.'

'I fancy Balmoral.'

'But so do I.'

'We'll have to toss for it.'

'Which do you want: heads or tails?'

'Heads. Best two of three.'

'Or three.'

'That's against the odds. You go first. Then it's my turn.'

'Okay. Here goes.'

'Heads! I get the first one. Now it's my turn. One, two, three, up!'

'Tails! One each. So who does the third?'

'Oh you. Maybe I'll do better if you toss it.'

'Heads! I get Balmoral.'

'Well I absolutely refuse to live in Buck House. Victoria Station I ask you. Dawn among the pavvies. Smelly bundles in every doorway. Imagine if you weren't in a car and had to walk past them. Anyway London terrifies me with all the riots. It's not safe either. Didn't someone get into Great Grandma's bedroom once?'

'Mummy and Daddy say they're retiring to the Isle of Wight, to Osborne. So you could have Sandringham.'

'You get a castle and all I get is a stately home.'

'Well, I will be queen of a whole federation. And I'll have to be woken up every morning by a bagpiper.'

'I love the bagpipes!'

⚜ ⚜ ⚜

AD 665

Although I only had the privilege of knowing him for a few short years, yet I wish to set down all I remember of our Father Aidan, who came to us by the will of God. So of his first coming here in Northumbria I will tell you as I heard it. It was in the year of Our Lord 634 while I was still living in the world. In the year before all of Northumbria, both Deira and Bernicia, lay under the cruel hand of Cadwalla, King of the Britons, and this the Lord had allowed to come to pass because of the apostasy of Osric and Eanfrid, both of whom had been baptised into the faith while they were living in exile among the Hibernian Scotti, but had reverted to idolatry as soon as they returned to their kingdoms.

After the death of Eanfrid, Oswald his brother, who had also received the faith whilst in exile, gathered an army of Christ's believers which, although small, was able to defeat Cadwalla's great army under the sign of a cross which Oswald had set up. Within a very short time following his victory, the king sent to Hy while Segenus was ruling as abbot, asking for a bishop to be sent to him to teach the faith to himself and his people.

Accordingly in answer to the King's plea a man was sent to them who was of a stern and unbending nature. Having no success he returned to the island saying that the people were too hard of heart to receive the Word, and were unruly and savage. So a great conference was summoned to decide what was to be done. Then Aidan, who was one of those attending, said to the brother priest whose mission had failed: 'Perhaps you were too hard on them from the beginning and did not do, as the Apostles, to bring them on slowly along the way with gentle words, easing them into the knowledge and the higher teachings of the lord by simple steps.'

Then everyone looked towards him and realized the truth of his words, and that this was indeed the gentle path to salvation, as a young kid first takes its mother's milk and only later learns to digest coarse food. So they saw that he was the fit person whom God had chosen to gentle these hard hearts, and consecrated him bishop. So he set forth from Hy, taking with him such of the brothers whom the Lord moved to go with him into those pagan lands, through the lands of the Picts, and then South by boat to the Saxon Kingdom of Northumbria, where the King, Oswald, conferred upon him the island of Lindisfarne to be another holy island, seat of the faith like Hy. And there he built his monastery and set about the teaching of those people.

From that time on Bishop Aidan worked tirelessly to bring the word of Christ to the lands under Oswald's rule, helped by the King himself with translation for the bishop did not speak their tongue while the king had leant Aidan's perfectly while in exile. And always Bishop Aidan spoke with the same gentleness so that all who heard him loved him.

Then through the King's bounty many churches were built and endowed and many priests and monks came from Dal Riata to baptise the people and work amongst them, so that both rich and poor gladly heard the Word and were baptized, and received into the monastic life.

So great was the respect for Bishop Aidan, for his wisdom and understanding, that when he summoned me to him I went gladly. I had decided that God was calling me to devote my life to Him as my sister, Herewith, had done after a life in this world, as wife and mother to kings among the East Angles. I had gone to that province to prepare to join my sister in the monastery of Chelles in Gaul, and had waited a year in preparation when I received the call from Bishop Aidan to return home.

When I came into his presence I prostrated myself before him but he, gently raising me up, motioned me to sit while he explained that he believed that the Lord had work for me nearer home. Then we prayed together that God would make clear to me his will in this matter and as we prayed a sweet conviction came upon me that this was indeed his will that I should minister among our own people.

So it followed, when Bishop Aidan was sure of my resolve, that I was granted an acre of land where I could perfect my understanding of the monastic rule, among a small group of companions and, after a year, I was made abbess of the monastery of Herutu following the departure of the holy nun Heiu to set up a monastery in Kallcacaestir, and she had been the first woman in Northumbria to be clothed and take her vows from Bishop Aidan himself.

Over the years I was visited often there by Bishop Aidan and others, with advice and expressions of understanding, as I myself grew in knowledge, until in time after Bishop Aidan's going to his heavenly kingdom I removed to

Streanaeshalch to found a monastery of monks and nuns there in a secluded place beside the sea, where we could be entirely devoted to the Word without the distractions of this world. And there were neither rich nor poor among us for I established from the beginning that we should hold everything in common.

❧ ❧ ❧

202?

Paul is giving the last touches to her setting up before the grand opening tomorrow. The central panel of the mural is covered by a curtain. Its drawing aside will be the climax of the ceremony, like the champagne bottle swinging against the new ship's side before it slides down the slipway into a maiden voyage. The side panels are already on view, whetting, she hopes, the appetite of visitors as they come into the atrium.

She is waiting for the removal workmen to bring across the last statue. The doors are pushed open and it is half dragged, half wheeled in under its all enveloping shroud.

'Over here,' Paul says, guiding them towards the plinth ready and waiting to be crowned with the draped figure.

'I'll just set up the hoist, miss. It's a heavy one, this. No mistake. Now then, gently does it. Kevin you take that side to steady it while I fix the hoist. Okay. Now then slowly. Don't let it swing. Just up enough to clear the trolley. Davey, help me position over the what's it. That's it. Now, hold her steady while I lower it. Right! Done! Stand back lads while I undo the hoist. Now move it back outa way. Right, Missus. That do?'

'Great! Well done. Thanks a lot.'

'Let's have a shufty then after all that.'

'You want to see her? Okay.' Paul steps forward. 'I'll get that box to stand on.'

Kevin brings over the box. Paul climbs onto it and gently tugs at the curtain until it falls away.

'What's it called?'

'She's the Abbess Hilda. A very powerful woman in her day.'

'When would that be?'

'About the middle of the 7th Century. 660ish.'

'And where was she from?'

'From Northumbria. Her father was related to the king.'

'There was a king in Northumbria?'

'Oh yes. Lots. That one, I think, was called Edwin.'

Kevin said: 'And she was called Hilda? So that's where it comes from. Me mam's called Hilda. She's never much liked it. You wait till I tell her.'

※ ※ ※

The opening had gone smoothly; the curtain had slid back to sighs of relief at the touch of the button. There was a gasp as the image came into view and then a round of applause. Paul had been warned she would have to be presented to the queen.

'Do I curtsey?' she asked Terry.

'Don't you dare!' had been the answer.

'Will you come with me?'

'Not to meet the queen. It's your day. Anyway we don't want to give her any shocks. I hear she's rather traditional.'

The chair of the commissioning committee was coming towards them. 'If you could come now Paula, her majesty wants a guided tour.'

'Good luck,' Terry whispered. 'See you later.'

A small party of local and regional dignitaries making up the entourage had assembled for the tour.

'She's only a kid really,' Paul thought as the queen put out a limp, gloved hand.

'Now you must tell me all about it, what you were thinking of, what it all means. I'm not used to modern art. We've lots of pictures but they're all old, mostly portraits. The interesting ones got given to the nation because we couldn't afford to protect them in London, and there wasn't room at Sandringham, and anyway that wouldn't have been any better. The poor security people have had a hard enough time protecting me. They're so afraid I'll be kidnapped like my aunt.'

'That must be very worrying for you ma'am,' Paul said.

'Oh it goes with the job. You get used to it; always having bodyguards around you. That's them over by the door. I told them to stand back while we go round. Can I call you Paula? Now what's this?'

'It's a statue of Abbess Hilda.'

'You see that's why I need help with modern art. I wouldn't have guessed in yonks. But I do know about her from history. She was a royal like me but not in the line of succession. So her only option was to go into the church, be a nun. That's right isn't it? Thank god times have moved on. I'd have hated to live then. She hasn't got a face. Why's that?'

'So everyone can imagine it for themselves. No one knows what she really looked like so we make her what we want her to be. She was very strong and admired for her wisdom, and everyone will see that in a different way.'

'And her habit? What is it just a sort of lattice, or rather a series of rods, iron or bronze?'

'Bronze, so it reflects the light, and I wanted the light to shine through the folds, nothing too heavy.'

'Now that mural I understand: that's the workmen building this place. Can I ask you something in strictest confidence while the others can't hear? I feel I can talk to you.'

'Of course.'

'I don't think Sandringham is a good idea for a royal residence. I thought it was at first but I was wrong. It's too cut off; nearly in the sea and miles from anywhere. I wondered about Blenheim. It's handy for London when I really have to go there, as I do quite often. And it's a palace just like my twinny's got at Holyrood.'

'You seemed to be getting on very well with HM.' Terry said when they were back at the hotel where they were spending the night.

'She's really just a kid. She wanted my advice about where she should live. She's thinking of moving to Blenheim Palace.'

Terry laughed. 'Well that would be in a royal tradition. Get a duke to build a spanking great palace and then take it over. Though it's best to get the old one to burn down first.'

❧   ❧   ❧

The twelve members of the Northern Assembly Council are meeting in the inner sanctum of the Council Chamber. This week Wolverhampton has the chair.

'Now that we've finally managed to wrest the right to raise taxes from Westminster we can start to really plan the future. So, suggestions.'

'Well, what's left of the coal won't last long. Energy is what we need.' Nottingham said. 'Can we get more wind-farms on the peaks?'

'We can but there'll be a fuss from the tourist trade and the environmental lobby.'

'I think we should look round to do a deal with one or more of the gas producers, like the Federation or Greenland.'

'The trouble with that Leeds is that then you're at their mercy, pricewise, and they can simply cut off the supply. Better Greenland than the Federation,' Manchester said. 'They're not empire building.'

'We could build a Tanker depot,' Newcastle offered.

'That's if the Scands haven't commandeered the lot.'

'Enough already. We'll never get anywhere like this. I propose we commission a feasibility study; look at all the options. All in favour? Anyone against? Good. I move next business. Liverpool?'

'We need something to pull us all together. Building the Assembly and the election of representatives, us, did it to start with. But now we need to follow that through.'

'Okay. Suggestions.'

'What we've all got,' Bradford said, 'is either an arts centre or a university or both. And we've got theatres, Opera North, the Halle, Liverpool, Birmingham orchestras. We cover all the arts and pop too. We should use these as the basis for a multi-cultural, multi discipline festival to showcase our identity.'

Stoke thumped on the table. 'That'd show them down South.'

'We can get together with Loughborough,' Leicester said, 'art, science, technology and sport. And then business will sponsor it all.'

'Now you're talking. How about: <u>Northern Lights</u> for a title?'

⚜ ⚜ ⚜

Paul and Terry are in bed together. You want to know what they do? You want to be Actaeon coming upon Diana or Vulcan lifting the sheet over Venus while Mars skulks under the bed? You want to look through the keyhole? You want to know where their hands go? They make love. What else? They fold their naked flesh together. Jealous?

❦ ❦ ❦

Terry pushed open the door to Paul's garden studio. It was rare for her to interrupt a working session. Outside sun was pouring into the garden making the blue hydrangea sing a deeper tone. Blue tits had flicked away from the nut-feeder as she had passed, chattering their disapproval.

'What's up?' Paul put down her brush.

'I've just had a call from Bob's office.'

'So?'

"He wants me to go in to number ten.'

'Does this mean what I think it means?'

'Maybe.'

'Well go and find out.'

'Give me a kiss for good luck.'

'Oh you! Any excuse…'

Terry sat on the train telling herself not to assume anything. It could just be for a chat. Surely it was too soon after her return to politics.

'Good. I'm glad you could come over,' Bob Stiles said waving her into a chair. 'I want you to work on a project in strict confidence. I don't want it scuppered before we've thought it all through. There will be enough opposition when it finally comes out, I mean when what I have in mind is made public, and I don't want it to be killed off in infancy. Sorry I'm being rather metaphorical and you haven't the least idea what I'm talking about. Well, another metaphor: I want to consider how we might put humpty dumpty together again. Do you know what I'm talking about, Terry?'

'I think so. You mean…'

'Don't even say it.'

'If you're thinking what I think you're thinking isn't that just 'perfidious Albion' again?'

'But this time it'll be different. Look if we don't do something the North will go next, and we'll be out of office forever.'

'Why me?'

'It needs someone with a brain and a long view. An historian in fact, who knows how we got here, and how we might go forward with the benefit of previous history. What will work; what will engage the public imagination and silence the doubters. You've seen it from the inside, and with your perspective you can also see it from the outside. You'll need the authority to go anywhere, talk to anyone. So I'm offering you a ministerial job in the foreign office, with special responsibility for cultural links, what used to be done by the old British Council. You'll need some assistance but it must be leakproof.'

'That sounds like good enough cover,' Terry said. 'And no one needs to know what's really underneath.'

'That's it exactly. You'd better have a quick trip somewhere to establish your credentials.'

'Oh India, I think. Cultural trade and so on. India's always good for that.'

'I'll let Max know you're to be given a free rein, so he won't think he can use you as an extra hand for a lot of routine foreign office stuff.'

'Can you do that without making him suspicious?'

'Oh I think so. The cultural side has been rather neglected. Everyone's been too busy trying to persuade the money brokers to set up shop again. I think they've gone for good. Now we have to find other ways. London's become the poor relation with Northern high-tech companies starting to set up and funnel the profits from our cheap property and labour back to their communal wallet. It's our own fault, the result of years of patronising neglect. And now we're just hanging on by our finger nails.'

'Well we've been here before and come back from it.'

'How so?'

'After the Romans left.'

Bob Stiles laughed. 'You see. I told you you were the right person.'

'Well?' Paul was in the kitchen when Terry got back, still feeling a little shaky. 'Do we open the last bottle of Prosecco?'

'If you like. But I'm only a junior minister! How do you feel about a trip to India?'

⚜ ⚜ ⚜

AD 665

During what were to be the last years of Bishop Aidan's earthly life, and before I came to Staeanaeshalch to found this monastery, the kingdom of Northumbria, which King Oswald had united, was again divided into two parts: the one, Bernicia, was ruled by Oswy while the other, Deira, was that of Oswin of Edwin's royal line, my kinsman. But although they were related by blood they were different in every respect. Oswin more resembled the pious and mighty prince, Oswald, the friend of Bishop Aidan, before him, while Oswy more resembled that Penda, the pagan king of the Mercians who had killed Oswald in battle in the ninth year of his reign.

As it had been with King Oswald so it was with Bishop Aidan and King Oswin, for the bishop was often at his royal palace of Bamburgh. On one occasion the king had given the bishop a fine horse to carry him for he was advancing in years, yet still travelled many miles on foot into the surrounding country preaching and baptising the people. Not long after when the bishop met a poor man who asked him for alms the bishop at once dismounted, and gave the horse with all its royal trappings to the poor man, for it was his custom to be always compassionate to the poor and kept nothing for himself of the gifts that rich men and princes bestowed upon him.

Hearing of this, King Oswin, as they were going to eat at the palace, asked why he had given the horse away, which he had intended for the bishop's own use. To which Bishop Aidan replied: 'Are you saying, Your Majesty, that that child of a mare was more valuable than a child of God?'

Aidan sat down at the table but the King, who was cold from hunting, warmed himself in front of the fire while he meditated on the bishop's words. Suddenly he unbuckled his sword and knelt at Bishop Aidan's feet, promising never to question him again about what he did with the King's gifts.

Bishop Aidan raised him from his knees, assuring him of his love and urging him to sit and eat which the king did, now laughing among his men. But Bishop Aidan grew suddenly sad and began to weep, and when his chaplain asked him why in their own tongue so that the others could not understand, he said that he feared such a king could not live long, 'because this people is unworthy of him.'

And so it was, for Penda again led a host against the kingdom, threatening to slaughter every one and remove the Kingdom of Northumbria from the face of the land. He laid siege to the castle of Bamburgh itself, piling great heaps of wood against the walls which he had taken from the surrounding villages, doors, beams, wattle walls, rafters and thatch, and as soon as the wind blew seawards he set fire to this mass, hoping to burn down the walls which had held him at bay.

At this time Bishop Aidan was on Farne Island to which he often retreated to pray alone in his hermitage with only the seals and the seabirds, God's creatures, for attendants. Seeing the smoke and flames rising above the city walls he raised his hands in prayer. At once the wind changed direction and blew the flames back upon the attackers, injuring some and driving the rest to flee and abandon their assault upon the city. Such was the power of Bishop Aidan's prayers.

⚜ ⚜ ⚜

202?

The quick trip to India was over. While Terry had visited local dignitaries in Mysore and Kerala, Paul had wandered through the streets and bazaars, besieged by small boys begging for money and cigarettes, delighting in the flurry of images and colours. Their hotel had been built in colonial times and still flaunted a huge ballroom floored with English oak, imported, shipped across the seas on what must have been a wave of extravagance so that officers in bright tunics could hobnob with princely families while dancing girls in gleaming silks swayed and gestured with delicate bangled arms. Paul almost felt she could see them still and hear the music. Once she climbed the hill above the little city to where the huge statue of Nandi squatted on the hillside, and watched as groups of women, mothers and daughters, aunts and nieces came to hang garlands of flowers like butterflies, between the great bow of his horns, and round the muscular neck.

Now they were back home and picking up on the email slurry that always forms in absence. They had promised each other not to look at them while they were away.

'Anything interesting in your lot?' Terry had asked. 'Mine are all PQs and committee minutes and reports, as well as a few constituency queries.'

'There's something here from a new group; the Committee for the Northern Lights, they call themselves. Looks like they're planning a cultural festival. They want me to go up and talk to them.'

'What do you think?'

'Could be interesting. I was wondering quite what to do next.'

'Do they mention a fee?'

'No. But it depends on what they want. I don't mind a chat. They'll pay my expenses.'

'It could be very useful, I mean, selfishly, to me. Bob Stiles thinks we could lose the North if something isn't done. They're on the up. It's history repeating itself, with all the manufacturing towns and cities being the powerhouse for the whole economy, the whole country in the 19th century. You could pick up their mood, what they're feeling, their intentions. It'd feed into what I'm thinking. But only if it suits you, of course; if it's something you want to get involved in.'

'I'll see how it goes. No promises.'

'No promises.'

It was a strange sensation to be confronted by her own work, now distanced by time and place. The statue of Hilda had found a new home, commandeered by the museum at Whitby but the murals still looked down from below the glass atrium. This time instead of a commissioning committee there was an assemblage of what Paul thought must be a mixture of councillors and executives from the towns, cities and countries.

'Good afternoon Miss Sanderson. Do take a seat. I'm Henry Cockburn, representing the Northumbrian County Council. Good of you to come.'

Paul inclined her head with a smile. Henry Cockburn went on, 'I expect you're wondering what we've got you up here for Miss. Look d'you mind if I call you Paula? I'll find it easier to get out what we want.'

'That's fine by me.'

'And I'm Harry. You see Paula we want to stage a big festival across the region to celebrate taking charge, now we've got the assembly, and next year we get to raise our own finances. We want to celebrate.'

'I think that's a great idea. But why me? I'm not an administrator, I'm an artist.'

'It's because of what you did for the Assembly building itself. Suddenly seeing your pictures I got it. It were the first time I understood what I were seeing, looking at a piece of art. You understand what we're about, and you can show others. I suppose that's what the artist's vision is, but until I see your things you did for us, I never knew. And people here feel the same. We need to look through your eyes for this. Isn't that so?'

There was a nodding and a murmur of agreement from round the table.

'But I'm not an administrator,' Paul said again.

'We don't need you to be. We can supply all that, give you a back up team. We want you to be the cultural or artistic adviser. We want your ideas, your vision. Anything you like to throw at us. And we want your advice on the projects that come in. Because we're going to ask for people to come forward from all across the region. Dance, music, theatre, exhibitions, poetry and so on. What do you think?'

'Sounds exciting. But a lot of work. One thing: perhaps because I've just come back from India, and a good proportion of people here have their roots in that part of the world. I think it would be very important to have their contribution to as many of the art forms as possible.'

'But not to the exclusion of our own stuff,' someone put in.

'Of course not. I was at the folk concert for the opening. I would definitely look for projects that reflected the area and its history. Whatever you might have thought of my sculpture of Hilda you can't say she wasn't one of yours.'

There was laughter round the table. 'About the logistics,' Paul said, 'If I were to take this on, I would want to be able to work mainly from home, in my own studio. Projects could be submitted in electronic format initially.'

'We'd like, shall we say, monthly meetings and updates.' Harry Cockburn said.

'That could be managed. I'd probably need some secretarial help, based up here.'

'We'd provide that and an office. So what do you think? We'll put it all in writing and give you a week or two to consider.'

'Just how long have we got?'

'A twelvemonth.'

'So we'd better get started.' The councillor from Manchester said.

Paul stood up. 'I'll wait for your letter.'

'It'll be in the post tomorrow. A proper contract,' Harry Cockburn said, shaking Paul's hand.

✤ ✤ ✤

'My turn to ask,' Terry said, 'so how did it go? What did they want?' She had broken out the two glasses and bottle of Pinot Grigio as soon as she got Paul's message that she was nearly home.

'They want me to advise them on a big festival they're setting up across the region. It's to celebrate having the power to raise local taxes or something like that.'

'And when is it supposed to happen?'

'Next year.'

'So they must be pretty sure of getting it through the final vote next week. And it's always the last step before some form of independence. Look at Wales.'

'But haven't some of the Welsh always wanted it? They've always seen themselves as a distinct people with their own culture.'

'Yes of course, like the Scots and the Irish. And now the Cornish. But this is England itself falling apart. How far can it go? Back to the Heptarchy?'

'What was that?'

'The Anglo Saxon Kingdoms; Mercia, Northumbria, Wessex and so on, that Aethelstan and Alfred finally managed to make into one, until the Danes messed it all up again.'

'That couldn't happen could it; all those different little countries?'

'I don't think so. But we could split North and South. The Germans and the Americans have more or less autonomous regions under a federal government but we're too small to go that far. It didn't even work in the so-called Dark Ages. And Ireland was as bad. All little kingdoms. That didn't work either. Now, everything's so globalized this fragmentation's even crazier. We're sleepwalking into something very nasty. Oh I'm sorry! Forget me ranting on. Will you do it?'

'I think so. As long as they really do agree to what I said I wanted.'

'Does it mean you'll be away a lot?'

'I've said a monthly meeting, and otherwise I work from home.'

'Oh good. I was so afraid you'd be away a long time.'

'Like Glasgow you mean. But at least we could be together a lot up there, with the cottage. I wasn't going to risk leaving you here with a lot of randy MPs and your constituents, and you propping up the Strangers Bar every night.'

'Good. But anyway I think I might be coming up there myself quite a bit if Bob Stiles has his way.'

⚜ ⚜ ⚜

'We can't hang about waiting for the cities, London and Westminster, to rescue us because they won't. We're on our own,' Islington said. There was a murmur of agreement.

'That's right. That's why I thought we should meet, by ourselves, just the boroughs. We can't make more of a mess of it than they have, running after the old fantasy of the city as a great financial hub. That's gone forever.'

'It's alright for you Christine, up in Harrow. At least you see a bit of the action when the businessmen fly into Northolt before heading straight to Birmingham and places North where the action is. You should come South of the river and see what it's really like,' Errol from Southwark said.

'Come on now, let's not start the old North and South of the Thames divide or we'll never get anywhere. At least that Hub has brought jobs and money. That's what we need more of. How do we go about it?'

'We need more foreign investment,' the gentle voice of Tower Hamlets put in. 'Let me tell you what we are doing. You know we have large communities from the sub continent. Fabrics are a traditional industry, as it once was in our area before, but then most of the clothing factories were Jewish owned, until the Second World War and the East End blitz. We are bringing that back with money from Indian investors, where the people still have connections with the family there and they have made good.'

'So on that basis the Chinese buy into Soho. The Hong Kong bank is there already, the Russians take over Paddington around Moscow Road, the Turks have Dulwich and so on. But what do they do?' Hammersmith was sounding frustrated.

'They invest in the area through the local council or if the enterprise is big enough, like Northolt, the business itself, and we use the council tax money as direct grant for business set-ups. We bring back industries to London that died out under the dead branches of finance that poisoned all the ground underneath as the ash tree does.'

'Or did; there's not many left now. I always wondered if that was just a myth.'

'Well it's a brilliant image anyway. And we'll set up our own chamber of commerce and community finance for the boroughs, and when the cities see how successful we are they'll want to join.'

'What about our own local banks?'

'If they want in they'll have to abide by the rules: no more sterile fantasy schemes of swapping debt. There has to be an end product. Not just mythical figures on a spreadsheet. And we'll set up a central bank to handle our own resources for the boroughs. We could give council tax payers shares, every borough a cooperative.'

'And we'll pass on contacts to each other and not just hog them for ourselves even if we can't use them. We'll need an office, a coordinator and a small staff to start with. Where shall that be?'

'Okay,' said Sanjay a councillor from Poplar. 'I will make the first gesture of solidarity. I suggest Wembley or Harrow so we can catch the businesses as they fly in, our gilded birds of many colours, and before they catch train out.'

⚜ ⚜ ⚜

'I want to know what the London boroughs are up to,' Bob Stiles said.

'What makes you think they're up to anything?' Terry asked.

'They're too quiet for a start, during the joint update meetings and Christina Willis who represents Harrow looks positively smug. I know they've set up a consortium to develop the Northolt Hub area. But it's more than that.'

'When I was in Bangalore talking to the local officials, I was told local businessmen were buying into the East End, reviving the garment industry. Is that possible? Wresting it back from China and Turkey and even India itself?'

'Why don't you get down there and see what you can suss out. Use your trip to India as an excuse. Go and see Sanjay Patel. He's very courteous, not frightening like some of our councillor colleagues.'

Terry came up out of Whitechapel station into another world from the one she had left at Stockwell, but now familiar to her from their recent stay in India, with its coloured ribbon of sari shops, interspersed with halal butchers and fruit stalls. Passing Queen Mary's University with its constant ebb and flow of students through the double doors, Terry walked down Bow Road to the art deco façade of the old Poplar Town Hall decorated by its carvings of labourers and craftsmen celebrating part of labour history, and now, like other town halls, sold off to private business.

This wasn't the Bow of Bow Bells but of Chaucer's French speaking abbess with her little dogs, and of the Yardley factory's mosaic of lavender sellers guarding the bridge. Sanjay Patel had an office in a converted warehouse where he attended to his own affairs when he wasn't required to sort out those of the borough. 'Coffee? Or tea?' he asked when they had shaken hands.

'Whatever you're having,' Terry said.

'Oh definitely coffee to keep me awake.'

'Where were your parents from? I've just made my first visit to India. I found it fascinating.'

'Where did you go?'

'Oh just Bangalore and roundabout. It wasn't a holiday you see.'

'Next time you must start at the top and work down. I recommend a minimum of six weeks. My parents were from Gujerat via Uganda. Ah here's our coffee. May I give you some? With milk? So what were you doing in Bangalore?' Patel asked when the door had closed on the young man who had brought the coffee, and he had taken his seat behind a large mahogany desk.

'Trying to drum up trade.'

'And did you succeed?'

'To a certain extent. The problem is that other countries that used to be called 'developing' have now overtaken us and can perfectly well do for themselves what we might have sold them.'

Sanjay Patel laughed. 'The fate of empires.'

'And you? How do you see your business developing? This is a pretty deprived part of London. While the Northern businesses have got themselves together with new technologies and old skills we're lagging behind.'

'Perhaps we are about to catch up.'

'You, yourself, you can see a future?'

Sanjay Patel steepled his fingers together. 'Yes, I see a future. I too have been to India recently, and now my order book is full, and I have acquired new premises and am hiring new staff.'

'And are you prepared to tell me the secret of your success?'

'Classic English style and fashions. The answer is not to import saris and Nehrus as in the past. But to export the tailored clothes that top- end market buyers want.'

' Could such an idea be translated into other areas?'

'Oh I am sure they are working on it. Our new London Chamber of Business is determined to succeed, and since the city can no longer finance us we must look elsewhere. For example the Saudis are interested in the old film studios. They will make movies for the whole of the Middle East, in competition with Bollywood, who expect to retaliate by setting up here themselves. Tales of the British Raj!' He laughed again. 'I hear Abu Dhabi is interested in the work being done by London University's joint technology development centre. And so on. This is my city and we shall make it hum again.'

Terry stood up. 'That's all very encouraging. I'm afraid you'll be doing me out of a job Mr Patel. But I'm glad to hear it. Just one thing. Are local government involved in this at all, supporting the communities?'

There was a pause then Patel said, 'We are taking shares in these enterprises; a form of community cooperative, you could say.'

'And they've set up their own cooperative bank to handle the financial side, make loans and so on,' Bob Stiles said when Terry reported her conversation to him. 'That's all fine. But where will it lead if we don't give it a strategic push in the right direction? London is trying to pull itself up by its bootstraps but that mustn't lead to the old North-South, metropolitan-provincial rivalry. I want you to go up to the Northern Assembly and see what can be done. The code word is Humpty Dumpty. Will you do that?'

'Paula's been retained to oversee the Northern Lights festival so there's every reason for a visit.'

'It's clever of them to have thought of that as a regional glue. Maybe London and the South should be thinking along those lines.'

⚜ ⚜ ⚜

AD 655

Now I must tell you of the death of Bishop Aidan which happened this way in the year of Our Lord 651. King Oswin the friend of Bishop Aidan ruled the Southern Part of Northumbria, Deira whiled his brother Oswy ruled the North, Bernicia. It is said that when the blessed Gregory saw fair haired boys in the Roman slave market and enquired who they were, and where they came from, he was told that they were pagans from Britain, from Deira and he then vowed to send holy men to convert them and save them from Deus Irae, the wrath of God.

King Oswy was not content to rule only a part of the Kingdom and so he made war on his kinsman, Oswin who, seeing that his opponent's army was much greater than his own, disbanded his men and went to wait concealed in the house of a noble called Hunwald, whom he thought was a loyal friend. But Hunwald betrayed Oswin to Oswy, who ordered his commander Ethelwin to seek him out and kill him and his attendant.

When the news came to Bishop Aidan, that his friend King Oswin had been so treacherously murdered, he was staying at a royal residence outside the town of Bamburgh where he had a church and a lodging, for he had no possessions of his own, a practice which I too followed after his example, but moved from one royal residence to another, constantly preaching and teaching the people.

Borne down by sorrow at his friend the King's death, and the manner of it, he fell ill. Then his attendants made a tent for him against the West wall of the Church, and it was as he was leaning against the post, buttressing this wall, that he drew his last breath and left this earthly life. Some few years later when Penda, the pagan king of

Mercia, again rampaged through the countryside with fire and sword, burning down the village and church where Aidan had died, it was afterwards found that the beam he had leant against had alone survived the flames. So passed Bishop Aidan eleven days after the murder of King Oswin. He was loved by all for his learning, his care of the poor and sick, his gentleness that left no room for pride, conceit, anger or greed, and in his time those who had before lived in darkness were brought to a knowledge of those same virtues.

⚜ ⚜ ⚜

202?

'Are you up for a night at the opera?' Paul asked as the train carried them northwards through the length of Britain. 'I've just had a message saying Opera North are doing <u>King Arthur</u> at The Sage and I ought to go and see them.'

'Let's go then. How do we get tickets?'

'Comps at the box office.'

'Then it's definitely something we should do. Gateshead's great for me. I'll be on the spot for the meeting tomorrow. What will you do?'

'There's an arts group in Newcastle I can visit. It's on my list.'

'Is all this going to stop you doing your own work?'

'Don't worry; they want me to do that as well as the coordinating bit.'

'There's the three star Ramada. Shall we try that?'

'It's quite something,' Terry said later, looking up at the great glass beehive of The Sage arts centre as they joined the crowd beside the Tyne, flowing past the graveyard of standing stones and in under the panelled canopy, where their tickets were waiting for them. 'Time for a quick drink? Where's the bar?'

'It's like an update of the Royal Festival Hall,' Paul said when they had taken their seats. 'I don't know this work at all,' she went on opening the programme.

'Neither do I. But here goes.'

The lights went down. The orchestra struck up, ending the overture with warlike trumpet calls, and then the Saxons marched onto the stage to placate their heathen gods, Woden, Thor and Freya before doing battle with Arthur's Britons.

'Not much changes,' Terry whispered between scenes.

Then the Britons' trumpets were heard and the fight began. Triumphant Arthur can't decide whether to pursue, guided by the airy spirit Philadel, or by the earthy goblin, Grimbald, who lures them towards a bog.

Now comes Arthur's sweetheart, Emmeline, to be entertained by the country folk. The shepherds offer symbolic panpipes to the women but they refuse to take them until offered marriage as well. 'Father Freud would have appreciated that,' Paul said.

'Make love not war. What's next?'

'A frost scene,' Paul read from the programme.

'It's like a pageant, a pantomime, a spectacle. All dancing, all singing, shape shifting,' Terry said as they made their way back to the bar at the interval.

'It's giving me lots of ideas,' Paul said. 'In a way it's totally modern with it's use of mixed media. All those scene changes. Everything's constantly shifting. If you look away you miss something. Do you remember the opening of the London Olympics in 2012? That's what it reminds me of. Next we've got naked fairies trying to seduce Arthur, but he stays true to Emmeline, and Britons and Saxons are joined by their union,' Paul read. 'And then Merlin takes over.'

'I wondered where he'd got to. Drink up. There's the bell.'

The stage became a whirl of wind and water as Merlin conjured up a storm, and then grew peaceful again as an island rose through the waves, with Britannia enthroned in the middle, to celebrate the nation's wealth of natural resources, while a trio of farmers sang in the harvest home, with a side swipe at the parson's poll tax.

'Who's this?' Terry whispered as a soprano took centre stage in a gilded chariot drawn by dancing doves.

'It's Venus.'

'Fairest Isle all isles excelling,
Seat of pleasure and of love,' Venus sang.
'Venus here shall choose her dwelling
And forsake her Cyprian grove...'

Gentle murmurs, sweet complaining,
Sighs that blow the fire of love,
Soft repulses, kind disdaining,
These be all the pains you prove...'

Terry and Paul are holding hands.

❧ ❧ ❧

Next morning the automatic glass doors let Terry into the foyer of the Assembly Hall. By now she was used to seeing Paul's work which she had watched being created, installed in strange surroundings but she paused a moment to follow the course of the murals around the walls of the atrium.

'I have a Dr Terry Ellis here for the council,' the receptionist said when she had been checked, photographed and issued with a pass to dangle round her neck. 'Sixth floor.' She said to Terry, waving her towards a glass turnstile that swung open at a touch from the receptionist, while a bouncer stood by in case an alarm sounded as Terry passed through to the lifts.

On the sixth floor another receptionist in her smart navy uniform escorted her along a corridor to the council room. 'Dr Ellis,' she announced.

'Do come in Dr Ellis and sit yourself down.' The chairman stood up and waved Terry to a chair at the end of a long table facing the wall of windows so that the faces at the other end were blurred against the wash of light.

'Now we're not quite sure why you're here. We presume the PM has sent you. Perhaps you should fill us in.'

'He's concerned about where we're going, as a country. He wants your views.'

'Oh Westminster wants our views does it? That makes a change,' a man on the left side of the table said. 'Well that's one way of putting it, a typical soft soap London way. We like something a bit plainer, a bit nearer the truth. You're here to suss out our intentions. Whether we're going to do a Scotland.'

'Alright,' Terry said. 'London's not just Westminster you know. It's Hackney and Peckham; Shepherd's Bush and Tottenham. They've more in common with you than they have with Mayfair or Chelsea. Bob Stiles is concerned for them if you, as you put it, 'did a Scotland.'

'We built this country, and the empire, with our industries, our sweat while you in the South were living off your tenants in rural England. Then you decided to go for big business where you didn't need to get your hands dirty, and you thought you could keep us in our place till you were ready to dump us. Well we're still here and now it's our turn.'

'Now Eric, give Dr Ellis a chance.'

'As I understand it,' a woman the opposite side of the table said, 'you're wanting us to save you from yourselves.'

'Something like that,' Terry said.

There was a sudden ripple of amusement round the table and the mood lightened.

'Well, you've got guts coming up here. I'll say that for you.'

⚜ ⚜ ⚜

AD 665

Such was the love of all for Bishop Aidan that while he was alive the differences of observation between the Irish and Roman practices were tolerated, although sometimes it meant that Queen Eanfled and her attendants who still observed the customs of her native Kent which had been converted by Archbishop Paulinus and, under her priest Romanus, was keeping Palm Sunday while King Oswy himself was already keeping Easter after the Irish custom. When however Finan succeeded Aidan as bishop, a man given to anger and obstinate by nature and later Colman, the king began to be troubled by these differences and at last, together with his son Alchfrid, he decided to call a synod to debate the whole matter.

At that time Agilbert, Bishop of the West Saxons, was visiting King Alchfrid whose friend he was. This king followed the Roman custom having been instructed by the learned Wilfred, who had himself been to Rome and spent some time studying the faith under the Archbishop of Gaul. The king had given Wilfred a monastery and land at In Hrypum, and Agilbert made him a priest there at the king's request.

It was decided that this synod should be held at my monastery of Streanaeshalch which I was most willing to do. Accordingly I received both kings, Bishop Colman with his Iona trained clergy and Bishop Agilbert of the Roman tradition together with Wilfred and Romanus. For myself I had, together with my community, been dedicated by Bishop Aidan, and so followed the practice of Lindisfarne and Iona. And also visiting at that time was the venerable Bishop Cedd whom King Oswy had send at the request of his friend Sigbert, King of the East Saxons, to resume the work of teaching the faith, which had lapsed in that kingdom, and who acted as interpreter to both sides, having both Scottish and Saxon tongues.

So a great gathering of princes, nobles, and holy men renowned for their wisdom and learning, was assembled, led by the monks and nuns of our community all chanting the hymn to the beginning of all things, which the herdsman Caedmon had written in our tongue, inspired by a heavenly vision, who afterwards I commanded should be fed with the words of the gospels so that all who did not understand Latin should nevertheless be nourished by them.

Nu scylun hergan hefaenricaes Uard

Metudes maecti end his modgidanc...

Opening the synod King Oswy bound all to accept whatever decision should be reached as the true way, for, he said, that as all hoped to be at one in the same heaven so all should be as one in celebrating its sacraments here on earth. Then Bishop Colman was asked to speak. He cited the Apostle whom Jesus loved, St John, as the origin of our beliefs. Then the King asked Bishop Agilbert to explain his rite and its origin but he, not being fluent in the English tongue deputed Wilfred to speak in his place. This he did at great length, saying that the whole of Christendom, including Greece, Africa and Egypt, was agreed on the same rite except only the Scotti, the Picts and the Britons, and presenting many strong arguments for the Roman view.

Then Bishop Colman, a gentle man, spoke again, saying that he followed the teachings of the holy Colmcille of Iona whose many miracles were proof of his mission from God. But Wilfred countered that Our Lord had given his commission to St Peter saying, 'On this rock I will build my church and the gates of Hell shall not prevail against it,' and that Peter was Bishop of Rome and therefore theirs was the rite to be followed.

So King Oswy asked Bishop Colman if these were indeed Christ's words, and on his agreeing that indeed they were, 'Then,' said the King, 'it is this we must follow, or perhaps when I come to the gates of Heaven to which Peter holds the keys he will turn away and they will not open for me.

And I too with all my community decided to follow the agreed path but Bishop Colman was unable to accept it and, taking others with him who were of like mind, he returned to his native Scotia by way of Hy. So one faith and one practice prevailed throughout all the English Christian Kingdoms.

⚜ ⚜ ⚜

Epilogue

203?

'So they've finally sent their, what shall I call it: 'envoy', 'spokesperson'?' The Council of the Federation is meeting in Glasgow. The First Minister of Scotland is in the chair for such an important event. 'And they've been very canny in their choice of diplomat, as is only to be expected from Albion.' He consults his papers. 'Dr Terry Ellis, some-time MP for Argyll and Bute; did a degree at Glasgow, now junior minister for overseas developments. Well, well, well.'

'We're overseas development now are we?'

'You could say that. Some of us are over the Irish Sea.'

'Oh, very funny.'

'Listen. We knew this was coming. We've discussed it before but never come to a conclusion. Now we have to deal with it.'

'What do you think their line will be?'

'They want in. We know that. Everything Bob Stiles has said since he was elected has tended towards re-establishing some kind of unity.'

'What's the difference between that and union?'

'Every difference. You don't need internal passports to go from one bit of this island to another. But you keep your own identity.'

'I think we should have her in. At least hear what she has to say.'

'Any change must be on our terms, as I've said before, or I can't sell it to my voters.'

'I think we should see it as helping them out, coming to their rescue. They've made a right mouldy haggis of it on their own.'

'I'll get her in then. Agreed?'

There is a murmur and a nodding of heads. The delegates stare down at the table and fiddle with their ipads while Glasgow goes to the door.

'Come in Dr Ellis, and sit yourself down.'

⚜ ⚜ ⚜

Paul is meeting Terry outside Portcullis House where she has been reporting back to Bob Stiles. 'Safer than Number 10,' he had said, 'Won't give the media a whiff of anything.'

The tide and the river are at full, lapping greyly against the walls of the old Parliament. Crowds of tourists are snapping the faded relics of past pageantry or queuing for the tour of Westminster Abbey. It never ceases to intrigue Paul that so many still come but then she remembers Persepolis, the hordes of visitors in Athens and Rome, Cairo and Teotihuacan: all fallen Empires.

Suddenly Terry is beside her. 'How did it go? Do you think they'll bite?'

'Bob does. As long as we're careful and resist any calls for us to try and be the dominant partner.

'What would it be called?'

'Nobody's thought that far. It can't be any form of 'united states'.'

'The Federation of the Isles sounds good.'

Terry looks up at the statue of Boudicca. 'I wonder what she would have called it, if there'd been any such thing, instead of a lot of warring chieftains and their tribes.'

'The daughters look terrified, hanging on behind.'

'Mother and the girls, 61AD. She's very splendid whipping on the horses. You can almost hear the sound of their hooves and the chariot wheels. The only person, male or female, who ever sacked London.'

'Hitler had a pretty good try.'

'If I had a patron saint I guess it would be her.'

'She got a lot of people killed. And she didn't have a happy ending. I'd rather you didn't have to poison yourself.'

'Idiot!'

'Where shall we go now?'

"The world was all before them where to go

And providence their guide..."

'What's that?'

'The end of <u>Paradise Lost</u>. The English version of the Sistine Chapel.'

'I don't want paradise lost. I want us to keep it.'

'Well Milton didn't really think they'd lost it.'

'It just makes me remember a terrible painting by Masaccio where Adam and Eve are being expelled from the garden, and they're howling with pain and grief.'

'Milton doesn't send them off like that at all. He has them hand-in-hand wandering slowly through Eden.'

'That's more like it. Come on then. Let's find somewhere to eat. I don't think Providence is going to provide.'

'There's the Inferno and Paradiso in the Strand.'

'Sounds perfect.'

Printed in Great Britain
by Amazon.co.uk, Ltd.,
Marston Gate.